Something Fatal

Sarah Dale

Printed in the United States of America

This edition Printed, 2021

ISBN-13: 978-1-952667-60-2
AISN: 978-1-952667-59-6

Cover Art © *Janina Franck*, 2021
Editing © *Ellie Piersol*, 2021
Interior Design © *Foundation Formatting*, 2021
Author Photo © *@elliehelladay* 2021
Additional cover graphics and author photo design ©
@amyhanachan 2021

If you're reading this, you've found my hidey hole. I've been keeping journals of our adventures for more than three decades now, and up until last week, I believed them to be safely hidden in my home. Now, everything has changed.

It's not that I fear they will be discovered, rather the opposite. I fear they'll be destroyed, and the record of our life's work would simply disappear.

I'm putting them here for safekeeping. I've spent enough hours in this library to know what gets tended regularly, and what gets regularly overlooked. So if you're finding this now, you must be doing a deep clean or maybe, just maybe, the City has come together with the funds for a new building, and this one is being cleared out.

Do me a favor. Do what you can to keep these safe. Tuck them back away, or move them if you need to, but don't let them be destroyed.

And if it's you they're meant for, then, good luck, my friend. You're going to need it.

Prologue

1987 WAS A rough year. That was the year we lost both David's mom and Shelly, one of the sweetest, loveliest members of Lorraine's coven.

David's mom didn't recover well from her ill treatment at the hands of Jeanne, the Pilgrim who was operating under cover as a librarian. The magic itself that Jeanne used didn't harm her, but her body wasn't well enough to perform the running around that Jeanne had magically made it do, and it was all too much for her. She passed away in her sleep a few weeks later.

Lorraine had become David's official foster parent a while back, and I think even before then plans on how to make him a permanent member of the family had been made, but there would be details to untangle for months before it would all be settled.

We held a remembrance service for Donna on the last Saturday in April at Lorraine's house. Mr. Rakow and David had put their heads together and come up with a mix tape of Donna's favorite songs. It was an interesting mix of heavy metal, old country tunes by cats like Hank Williams senior and the Carter Family, and Cyndi Lauper.

I got the sense that David put more stock in the music than the gathering. He was pretty stiff all through it, even though it was mostly people we knew well: Mr. Rakow, Lorraine, the Coven and my folks. A few teachers and coaches from school came to show their support for David, which I thought was pretty great. It was all very informal. My dad said a few words, and Mr. Rakow told funny stories about when Donna had first moved to that house when David was a toddler running wild on the sidewalks in his padded pants and she would have to chase all over the neighborhood trying to catch him. Then we had iced tea and sugar cookies and the adults spoke in low voices meant to sound comforting and hugged David around the shoulders.

Afterwards the four of us took off in Jen's car, Clint. We drove out in the country. Nobody talked much, we just drove around for a couple hours. Finally, we drove through a fast-food place in a small town north of Lincoln, and sat in a picnic shelter at the town's one park and ate our burgers and fries. The sun was just disappearing over the horizon, its last red rays reflecting balefully off the metal slide in the play area.

We sat quietly for a while afterwards, everybody lost in their own thoughts. I'm not sure what anybody else was pondering, but I was thinking about my own mom, and how I would feel if something happened to her, which fell into the severely not good category. Then I tried again to imagine what it might feel like if my mom was more like David's mom.

To be honest, that's where things got super complicated for me. I was still pretty mad at Donna for anything and everything she'd done to hurt David, whether the abuse was delivered by some boyfriend, or by her own hand. I'd talked to my folks about it a couple of times, and they always said that Donna was as much of a victim in her life as she made David. I understood that, but it made my feelings even more confusing, especially now that she was gone. I couldn't figure out just how to hold my anger at her, and my sympathy for her all together at once, and now that she was gone, I felt like I'd missed an important deadline. The burger and fries were doing nothing to fill that particular emptiness in my gut.

"How do you feel? Do you want to go back to the house?" Jen asked when we were down to the last dregs of our sodas and the crunchy bits from the bottom of the fries container.

"I don't know." David sighed and scrubbed his greasy hands on his jeans distractedly. "I don't know how I'm supposed to feel," he said, poking his trash back into the bag and smashing it into a tiny ball.

I replied with something I'd heard my dad say to a friend who was going through a difficult time; "There's no rule book. Feel what you feel, tell us if you want, or don't. If you need help, ask. If we think you need help, we'll tell you. And eventually, it'll get easier."

David looked at me like he was trying to translate my words from the Greek. I leaned across the table and held up my hand. He gripped it. Jen and Jon joined hands with us.

"We got you, man," said Jon.

David released my hand and high-fived each of us gently. He picked up the compacted bag of fast-food debris, and chucked it at the trash can ten feet away. A rim shot, but it went in. We all trundled back to the car and went home.

Shelly had recently lost her mom, too. Her mom was elderly, and had been sick for a long time, but I don't think that matters too much when it's your mom. She and David connected strongly because of it.

At most of the Coven's non-work gatherings, of which there were plenty, Shelly was often the life of the party. She had the funniest stories, the most musical laugh, and she had a way of listening to whoever she was with that just made you feel really seen and treasured. It was at one of those backyard barbeques that she invited him to walk out at Wilderness with her and Tati.

Tati was Shelly's dog. She was this gorgeous little golden girl, "yellow" in dog breeding language. A Yellow English Lab. In normal person language, she was a golden-blonde, 40 lb. bundle of mischievous energy. She and David were two peas in a pod, running, exploring, goofing around. David adored Tati, and he was second only to Shelly in her doggy affections.

Those walks seemed to be good for him. Shelly seemed to be good for him. I got the impression that they talked some, and walked a lot. Generally, he came back from those walks seeming a little lighter.

So, when we lost Shelly too, David took it really hard.

On a slightly lighter note, Jon's vision had continued to evolve. Once the glasses failed to help at all, he entered a stage of complete visual darkness, and then it changed again. He became increasingly able to perceive shapes and motion, but the inputs had changed.

He said it wasn't the same as seeing with eyes. It was more like a full-body knowledge. "Like," Jon told me one sunny afternoon walking home from the 7-11 on the corner, "like, you know if you shut your eyes right now, you'd feel the sidewalk beneath your feet, you'd feel the sun warmer on your back than your front, you'd hear the traffic buzzing by on our right side, right?"

"Yeah," I'd said, closing my eyes and testing each of those perceptions in my own head.

"So, you sort of have this picture in your head, right? But it's sort of vague and choppy. Bits are missing. You don't know exactly where the seam in the sidewalk is pitched up because of the tree roots, or if the Miller kids left their bikes sticking out of the yard onto the sidewalk again today, right?"

"Right!" I squeaked, the toe of my sneaker catching

on a sidewalk seam and making me stumble. Jon caught me.

"So that's what's changing," he said. "Those blanks are starting to fill in, lighten up, seem more concrete. Like right now," he paused on the sidewalk, one hand in mine, the other clutching a 64 oz cola-flavored frozen Slurpee. "Right now, I can tell you that there's a wooden fence around the yard on our left, that we're in between a wooden house and the next one, which is brick, and that that there's a big elm tree in the yard two houses up on the corner."

I glanced around, super impressed, verifying all of that.

"But, I can also tell you that elm tree is sick. It's got some sort of critter eating at it, and the tree is dying." Jon gestured at the tree with his Slurpee.

I stared at the tree on the corner. "It doesn't look sick to me." I said thoughtfully, still innocent of the Dutch elm disease that would eventually eliminate most of the elms in Lincoln.

"I figured. Whatever I'm sensing isn't the same thing as what you see on the outside. I think, and mom thinks, what I'm seeing is more like the *essence* of the thing. Like, I'm sensing the life inside the thing. Wood houses have a different *essence* than brick ones, and healthy trees have a way different *essence* than sick ones."

"But you're not seeing at all through your eyes?" I asked, trying to understand.

"I don't think so. I'm pretty sure the eyeballs have been relegated to decorative status." He winked at me with one *very pretty* green eye. "Whatever the inputs are, it's mental or spiritual or magical, I don't know. It's in my head, and it's real, and the more I lean into it, and trust it, the better it works."

He would still sometimes *hitchhike* on one of the three of us, seeing and hearing with our eyes and ears, but this new sense was developing as well. He struggled a lot those first years after his sight changed. He couldn't drive, and that was a real blow to his independence. School became three times harder, suddenly. He had to have text books read aloud to him, and had to have an aide come and sit with him in class, to tell him what was being written on the chalkboard. The idea of going to college now seemed crazy complicated, and job prospects looked grim.

I did what I could to make it easier for him, especially school-wise, but the journey was very internal, and for a lot of it, he was on his own.

For my part, I'd spent the last couple of months immersed in a couple of major projects. One was a Summer Intensive class I'd lucked into on the Wesleyan Campus, and the other was a piece of research two of Lorraine's coven members were engaged in, trying to figure out more about the Astrological implications of the triad's power. Lisa had studied with Maka when she was in town, and Maka had set her on a path of inquiry. Nicole and I were acting as her research assistants; finding, reading and summarizing books and articles she assigned us, and reporting back.

Jen and David had decided to get the volunteer hours they'd need for senior year out of the way early, and were spending their mornings volunteering at the Humane Society. I have to admit, I was a little jealous I hadn't thought of that myself. I'd probably do my hours at the library, which seemed a little less exciting after Jen told me their plan.

But all in all, most of the excitement over the summer started innocuously enough, with being late for class.

Friday, June 12th, 1987

Hi 98°/Lo 68°

Sun ♊ Mercury ♋ Venus ♉ Mars ♋ Jupiter ♈
Saturn ♐ Uranus ♑ Neptune ♑ Pluto ♏ Moon ♐

I STEPPED OUT of the Old Main building on the Wesleyan Campus and squinted into the blazing Friday afternoon sunshine.

Barf.

It was grody hot. If Ken the weather guy was to be believed, it was going to be god-awful for the foreseeable future. At or near 100° for the next three days at least and now chance of rain until Wednesday of next week.

I stepped out of the flow of students into the shade of a nearby ornamental pear tree and dug around in my book bag for my sunglasses.

I was taking a six-week summer intensive on the Mysteries of Agatha Christie. It was a unique class, taught by a guest lecturer from Cambridge. A third of the 36 students were Wesleyan students. Another third were interested members of the community – I recognized a couple of Librarians in that group. And the final third of the class was high school students like me.

The opportunity to take the class had been presented to all Nebraska high school students in Advanced/Gifted English classes. If you were interested, you had to submit an essay on one of Christie's works and be accepted by a panel of Wesleyan English Professors. I was totally lucky to have gotten in.

I had to remind myself of that every time my alarm clock went off at 7:00 a.m. on another day of my precious summer vacation. I was running a little late that particular morning because I'd happened to see a car accident.

Some woman in a big fat hurry knocked down a guy on a bike and took off. The guy was okay, but I'd gotten the license plate, so I waited with him until the police arrived to take the report.

"A blue Volkswagen Beetle, with three-county plates," I told the officer, reciting the digits I'd jotted down in my omnipresent notebook. "There was a big dent in the rear bumper, driver's side. She was going really fast; this guy is lucky."

License plates in Nebraska used to begin with the County number. Back in 1922, the counties were numbered in order of their population, so Douglas County, where Omaha sits was number one. Lancaster county, which contains Lincoln, was number two. It went all the way to itty bitty number 93 with its 1,300-some souls within its 721 square miles. Number 93 was Hooker County, named for a Union General in the Civil War named Joseph Hooker, whose primary claim to fame was getting his butt handed to him by Lee at Chancellorsville.

Three county is Gage, home of Beatrice (emphasis on the AT), a town forty miles to the south of Lincoln, over the years, it's been home to a couple of authors, baseball players, one NFL running back, and the cinematographer who cooked up the parting of the Red Sea scene in *The Ten Commandments*.

"You have a sharp eye for detail," The officer told me.

I wasn't surprised. We'd been into clues and logic and motives and crime scenes so much over the last few weeks. I think all of us in class were walking around campus looking for mysterious pill bottles, scraps of paper with elegant handwriting, eyeing suspicious strangers and eavesdropping on conversations hoping for delicious snippets.

The class would be over with by next week. Some of the kids that had come from Omaha or other towns around were planning an end-of-class party in their dorm tonight. I'd considered going, but David, Jen and Jon all wanted to go see the new flick coming out that night, *Predator.*

I really had enjoyed the class, and the people. The curriculum had been insane, but awesome. Essentially, you had to show up having read all fifteen of the novels they were covering already. There just wasn't time to do so during the class. I trudged across campus, and across 56th street towards home.

The houses here, though less than a mile from my own, were quite different. The area around Wesleyan was a tiny island of 2-story frame houses and brick Tudors in a sea of post WWII ranch style development. It was a beautiful walk I'd have enjoyed far more if it wasn't freaking nuclear hot outside. I picked up my pace in the blindingly hot exposed places on the sidewalk, and lagged in the spots of shade cast by friendly oaks and elms.

A couple of blocks up ahead, where I was to turn right on 60th St. I spotted something that drew my eye. The house on that corner was set well back from the street and a split-rail fence surrounded the yard. Split-rail fences are made from old railroad ties, widely spaced apart. They're more a visual barrier than a physical one. A glorious, big, slinky black cat with a hot pink collar was stretched out on the precarious top rail like Cleopatra on a chaise lounge. I'd never seen this gorgeous kitty on my walk, and I wondered if she lived there.

The 4" wide wooden beam in the blazing sunshine didn't look too comfy to me, but then again, I wasn't a cat, and she looked happy so who was I to judge? I observed her interestedly for two blocks while I approached from the West. Interested, because I was always interested in cats. *Mildly obsessed*, is how Jen would have put it. If a cat was in the vicinity, it drew me like a magnet. The part time visits from Bast only whet my appetite. Stupid Mallory and her stupid allergies.

I promised myself for the thousandth time that the first thing I was going to do when I moved out was get a kitten. I amused myself for the remainder of that block, speculating on what color of fur my future kitty might have. Would she be black like this one?

The cat stretched out along the split-rail was black like the deepest corner of the moonless night sky. She seemed to absorb all the hot sunlight pouring down on her and transform it into a cool puddle of mysterious shade, silent and all but unmoving, save for the tiniest of tail twitches. As I got closer, I revamped my estimation of how big this kitty was. Bast was a pretty big girl, at least ten pounds. This kitty was even bigger.

About half a block away, I made to cross the street so I could walk by her and say howdy, maybe get in a head rub. My detour was cut short by a demanding, "Meeeoooowwwww!"

I stopped in my tracks. Bast's commands were unmistakable. I turned back in the direction I would normally take, and spotted her, sitting plainly in the middle of the sidewalk, halfway down the block. She seemed to be expecting me.

"Hey beautiful!" I greeted her. She observed my progress as I turned the corner and headed her way. She waited until I caught up, eyed me expectantly until I dutifully scratched the preferred spot behind her right ear, and then began gracefully walking towards my house.

I followed along. Since we were the only two brave souls abroad in the heat of the day, I unselfconsciously rambled along in one-sided conversation with her as we strolled home.

"What are you doing this fine day, Miss Bast? I know you love the heat, but this is usually one of the 20 hours a day that you nap! Plus, that Siamese coat is beautiful, but it's a tad warm even for you on a day like today. Not that I'm not just pleased as punch to have you walk me home, you know that."

"Mmrrph"

"Exactly! So, class was good today. We're finally finished with *all* the reading, so you won't' have my bookbag to snooze on in the den quite as much."

"Meow!"

"Oh, okay. I guess I could leave it down thee on the couch for you if you want?"

"Mrrph!"

"Yes, ma'am! But I'll put it in there later, okay? I need to haul butt over to Jen and Jon's. We're going to the movies tonight and I'm getting ready over there. I just have time to grab my other bag and go. I wish you could come inside the rest of the house. You could nap on my bed. Ugh. Stupid Mallory and her stupid allergies."

"Meowph!"

Bast walked with me until I got to my driveway, and then stopped in the deeply cool shade of the big old Douglas Fir tree that grew between our house and the neighbors to the west.

I curtseyed to Bast. Jen always said she looked like she deserved our veneration, so we'd either bow or curtsy when we saw her. Now she appeared to expect it and there was baleful glaring if the niceties were ignored.

I zipped into the empty house. My heart nearly stopped from the change of temperature from outside. I exchanged by book bag for my overnight bag and ran back out into the heat before my body could get too comfortably adjusted.

I saluted to Bast from across the front yard. She hadn't moved from the shady spot under the fir. She sat, gracefully composed, tail tucked around her toes, and watched me cross the street.

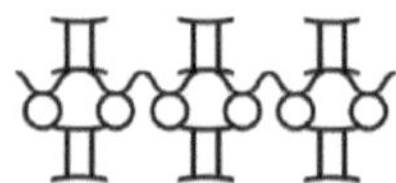

A HOT MINUTE later, I arrived in front of Jen's house. I'd just started up the driveway when the aura of trouble hit me like a brick wall. I paused mid-step and looked at the kitchen door where we normally went in and out. Closed. Kitchen curtains? Drawn. Could just be against the blazing sunshine, but no.

Lorraine's car. It was parked in the driveway instead of in the garage, and the garage door was down. I strained my ears to filter out the sounds of the half dozen or so air conditioners running nearby, keeping the neighbors' houses cool.

Most of the houses on this block of one-story ranches with central air conditioning. Window AC's weren't the norm. Just as I identified the distinctive sputter and clank of the giant window unit Lorraine had installed in the garage's one back window, the side door of the garage inched open and one hand appeared in the crack. Jen's elegantly long fingers graced by her sensationally long fingernails appeared. The pointer-finger stabbed directly at me, and then turned decisively up and gave the *come here* gesture. Then the hand disappeared, and the door closed.

Lorraine's garage was a master class in cleanliness, organization and multiple uses. She was, among other things, a leading Sage in the Garage Saleing Community. Online marketplaces like eBay were still years away. In June of 1987, if you wanted to sell your junk, you had to dedicate all your Saturdays to being present and organized in your garage from 6:00 a.m. to noon. This is when you'd play host to your neighbors, some wackier than others, and charge them 50¢ for a stack of paperbacks and $2 for an outgrown t-shirt.

The best ones offered something more and Lorraine used hers to showcase the Coven's handicrafts. Everything at her sales had a subtle witchy vibe to it, and while the items of real power were never sold to the uninitiated, her Saturday sales had a reputation for having great scented candles, tons of hand-knits, a little fresh produce and flowers from the garden, and exotic looking hand-made jewelry. A couple of the witches took turns doing an hour or so of Tarot readings on alternating Saturdays.

They also used the garage space for Coven activities. It could be closed up for privacy or opened to the elements in the fenced backyard as need for whatever spell they were working on. And when nothing else exciting was happening inside, it actually *gasp* due to Lorrainne's meticulous storage and design, housed her car.

I slipped in through the door Jen's had has just vacated, taking her cue and closing the door quickly against the heat.

The five people inside had turned the space into an impromptu command center with two square card tables surrounded by a scattering of folding chairs. One table held an untouched pitcher of iced tea which, judging from the intact cubes, hadn't been out here too long. The window AC was going on full blast, but it was a large space. The AC made things more tolerable than comfortable.

Seated around the nearby second card table sat Lorraine, Jen, and three of Lorraine's Coven members, Dorothy, Lisa, and Nicole. Lorraine had the cordless phone clutched in one hand and a pen in the other. She was taking notes as she spoke to someone on the phone

Jen also had a pen and was adding notations as Lorraine wrote. I noticed Jen's eyes were closed as she wrote, and felt the warmth of my necklace as its blue glow brightened in proximity. She was listening with more than her ears. I remained carefully silent so as not to interrupt her flow.

She and Jen occupied chairs at one corner of the table. Opposite them, also with their chairs drawn companionably close, sat Lisa and Nicole. Had gay marriage been legal in the 80's, I might call these two newlyweds. They'd been introduced by friends a few years back, but their romance hadn't blossomed until they began working together regularly as members of Lorrain's Coven.

They'd kept it all pretty low-key since it was, in a weird way, a work romance. The Coven, like any workplace was beaucoup packed with drama. Lorraine did her managerial best to ensure that the group functioned together as a team, but yeah. Drama.

In this particular case, the drama centered around Pat, another Coven member, with whom Nicole had a brief and somewhat steamy by all accounts, fling. Said fling began, existed, and ended some months before Nicole and Lisa began dating. Regardless of the timing their relationship effectively dashed any hopes Pat may have harbored of either a repeat performance, or more heartbreakingly, something serious.

Pat declared up and down that she was on board the happy train with the new couple, but it was pretty obviously forced. When Pat was around, I'd noticed, Lisa and Nicole kept more physical distance between themselves and maintained very relaxed, but work-like demeanor. When they were free of her presence, like now, they were more snuggly.

They sat, nearly facing one another. Lisa was a neatly structured person whose occasional unpredictability made her kinda awesome. She had perfectly respectable, shiny brown hair that framed a sweet heart-shaped face, deep brown eyes, and the turned-up nose of a deeply mischievous and scary powerful fae princess.

She'd just come from work, it appeared, as she was rocking her teacher uniform of tailored slacks, silk blouse and almost-sensible heels. At Lisa's side was her knitting bag, which she was never without. Today's creation was emerging from a heathered violet shade of yarn, it's final form still but a vision in her brain.

Connected to her by the skein of yarn sat Nicole. She was rolling the purple yarn up from the other end. A puddle of it lay unfettered in her lap. She rolled nervously, her fingers sometimes working manically, sometimes pausing entirely while she listened to Lorrain's end of the conversation.

Unlike Lisa, Nicole had evidently *not* come straight from work. I was familiar with her work outfits as she had just recently replaced Jeanne as Librarian at my neighborhood branch. She'd been unhappily working at the University Library for some time, so when the job came open, she'd gone for it.

While Nicole's black and flowing garb at work, along with her gorgeous handmade jewelry and arresting grey eyes had already lent a whole new vibe of mystery to the neighborhood branch library scene, her off-duty outfits were off the hook. Stevie Nicks would have been jealous. Today's skirt was layer upon layer of gauzy fabric in multiple shades of black, grey and purple. The top had sleeves that were more like wings, slit underneath to allow her bare arms to show. The bodice front was intricately embroidered and multidimensional with tiny stones and shiny copper bits sewn in. Bracelets lined her arms and rings covered her elegant fingers.

The final Coven member present was also the eldest. Dorothy, or Dottie as she was most often called, was probably in her mid-seventies then. She had a glorious crown of bright silver hair cut short in a pixie that suited her right down to her toes. She rocked serenely, listening closely and thoughtfully but without the worry that was clearly etched on the faces off the others.

Dottie had been Lorraine's right hand from day one. Dottie could easily, as the eldest and most experienced, have assumed the leadership role. But while she acted as Lorraine's de facto second in command, she had work that required her to travel, sometimes unexpectedly, and so she insisted that Lorraine take the helm.

I wasn't super clear on what exactly her current job was, but I knew from my dad that she'd retired from a professorship in the Art Department at Wesleyan some ten years ago. He said she was beloved by staff and students alike. It wasn't hard to see why.

I slid into the proffered chair next to Jen, opposite Dottie who smiled warmly and slid a glass of iced tea across the table to me. I accepted silently and gratefully. Good land it was hot outside. I raised my eyebrows Jen's way to get any more insight into whatever was happening here. She was completely focused on her mom's phone conversation. I tuned in as well.

"Has Shelly's librarian friend," Lorraine asked who-ever was on the other end, "argh, tell me her name again, Charlotte, right? Has Charlotte spoken with the police?"

I pricked up my ears and glanced at Nicole for con-firmation. She nodded in answer to my unspoken ques-tion. Miss Charlotte was a Librarian downtown. She and Shelly were best friends. I'd only worked with Miss Char-lotte in person a few times, but she was my phone go-to for research in the Periodicals Room. The Keeper of the Microfilm.

Lorraine went on, "Good. yes, I know Detective Rogers. She's great, and Officer Yardley speaks highly of her."

Office Yardley was our neighborhood police officer. It was he who had fought off the Great Dane-sized spi-ders that Jeanne had conjured. If this Detective Rogers was well thought of by Officer Yardley, it might mean she was one of the few who either *saw* the scary-weird stuff like we did, or at least wasn't fazed by it.

"Okay, keep us posted. Right. Same here." She hung up.

"Hey Angie sweetie," Lorraine said. Her voice sounded thin and tight. I smiled my patented, *Never fear, help is here!* smile at her. She returned it with her, *Oh boy, here we go again!* smile and looked around. "I've been on the phone non-stop for an hour and I'm parched! Some-one let me have some of that iced tea and I'll organize my notes while it's all fresh in my mind and let the others fill you in."

Dottie slid her a glass. Lorraine accepted gratefully and began a fresh page in her notebook. I glanced hopefully around at the others.

"Angie dear," began Dottie, sounding uncharacteristically hesitant. "One of our sisters, Shelly, has gone missing. She missed last night's meeting and no one has heard from her. We're trying to discover what's happened."

Here Nicole picked up the story. "I called Charlotte late last night. She and Shelly are close, and Charlotte dog-sits for Shelly whenever she has meetings out of town. I figured she'd have a house key, and she did. She went over first thing this morning." She sighed and glanced at Lisa, who nodded supportively.

"There was no sign of Shelly or Tati. The garage door was open and the kitchen door's knob was locked, but not the deadbolt." Nicole shook her head, trying to make sense of that detail.

I understood the worry. The idea that Shelly might have taken Tati and gone someplace and not told Charlotte could *maybe* happen, but in conjunction with missing a regular Full Moon meeting without saying anything to the Coven? Something was definitely hinky.

"Then Deanne got word from that chatty good-looking reporter she's friendly with. A car accident was discovered on East Campus. A driver ran off the road and crashed into Dead Man's Run. A woman's body was found," Nicole said, worry making her voice tight.

"When? Has the body been identified?" I asked, reaching into my overnight bag for my own pen and notebook.

"About 11:00 a.m. and no, they haven't yet," Jen replied. I studied her face.

"Are you getting any visiony help?"

"Enough to be bad, but nothing specific enough to be useful," she said frowning. "A feeling of fear and darkness, something sharp and something wet."

Oh crap. That didn't bode well at all, but still. "We don't know if the woman in the car accident was Shelly. She could be somewhere else, right? When was the last time anyone talked to Shelly?" I asked, scribbling notes.

My usual nerdy tendency to write everything down had been supercharged by my current Agatha Christie immersion, and I ran with it.

"Wednesday night," Lisa said decidedly.

"Yes," Nicole agreed. "Charlotte and Shelley had dinner together at Charlotte's house Wednesday night."

Nicole fussed with the yarn in her lap and looked up at Lisa, her brow furrowed, her eyes dark and troubled. "Charlotte said they had a fight about something. She said it was nothing serious, just Mars in Cancer making them both testy. She's really shook up about it. She said Shelly loaded Tati up around 11:30 p.m. an went home. She said she's sure Shelly got home because Tati's leash, the one she was wearing earlier, was hanging on its usual hook in the garage by the kitchen door."

Tati was Shelly's adorable yellow English Lab. English Labs were supposed to be less crazy and more trainable than American ones, but Labs are Labs. Effusively friendly, determined to be your favorite by hook or by crook, and always ready to run around and play.

If Shelly knew David would be home on Coven Meeting nights, she'd bring Tati. Jen and the boys and I would walk her over to Mr. Rakow's and pick up Shadow and take them over to play at the elementary schoolyard. The dogs could romp for hours there, and did.

Lorraine set her pen down on her notes and sighed. She looked to Dottie and asked, "Did Shelly have any other family? I got the impression that she moved back here to be with her mom since there was nobody else left."

"I don't think so," said Dottie. "I've known Shelly's mom for many years, and I think you're right about she and her mom being the last. Shelly never married or had any kids. I suppose there could be someone on her dad's side, but I don't know. He wasn't a topic of conversation with either of them."

Jen stood suddenly and went to the door. She cracked it, as she had for me, but this time she stuck her head out and yelled.

"We're in here, Rome, Jules!"

When Rome and Jules entered the garage, it felt like someone had dialed the energy reserves up to eleven. Rome came through the door first, face red from the heat, fanning herself mightily. She was sporting a sundress in bright jewel tones of her own design and construction, I was sure. She was a walking, singing, explosion of sunshine.

In my notebook, I jotted down, *Rome: 5'11, 32 yo wf, short blonde hair. Arrived with Jules at 5:45 p.m. 6/12/87 Jules: 6', 29yo wf, shldr leng lt. brn hr, drove car? Didn't hear cycle.*

Jules entered a step behind her, looking as beautifully disheveled as always – zero makeup, perma-bedhead, and laser bright icy blue eyes that conveyed an active interest in everyone and everything. Jules was working on her PhD in Geology and was the Coven's expert at identifying and using stones effective at amplifying or directing the Coven's magic.

Rome was the Assistant Manager at a café on the highway north of town. The owner had recognized her skills with design and had wisely hired her to re-vamp his plain diner's décor into something that would set him apart from the big chains that were taking over everyplace. She had redecorated the place and designed uniforms for the staff that turned the plain place into an homage to classic diners of the 50's and 60's. The customers loved it, the owner loved it, and she just went on being Rome, spreading sunshine and awesomeness like flower petals from a pixie's basket.

In the times I'd gotten to watch the Coven work magic together, Rome's magic always seemed to supercharge things. Also, she sang all of her spells, which was kind of fabulous to listen to.

Even their formidable combined energies dampened when they entered the garage.

"What's going on?" Jules demanded.

"We got your messages when we got home and we came right over!" Rome exclaimed. She'd made a beeline to Lorraine and gathered her in a huge embrace. Is there any word? Any new news?"

Lorraine accepted the hug as gratefully as I'd taken the iced tea earlier. It visibly recharged her. I wondered if that was a Coven thing or just a human thing.

"Nothing definitive yet. Grab a seat and a drink you two. I was just about to run over my notes from Deanne and what all we know so far." Rome and Jules brought over folding chairs and a third card table and settled in.

"We know the last time Charlotte saw Shelly was Wednesday night. They had dinner together at Charlotte's house. They had a disagreement; the nature of which Charlotte did not elaborate to Nicole."

Nicole shook her head, frowning. "She just said it was something dumb, but she sounded really broken up about it."

"We know that Shelly left Charlotte's house at 11:30," stated Lorraine, looking at her notes.

"Did she mention anything to Charlotte about where she was going? Did she intend to go straight home?" I asked, scribbling madly in my notebook.

Nicole shook her head. "I didn't ask," she said, "and I don't remember her saying, Angie." I nodded and scribbled.

Everyone there had known me long enough to know that writing was how I processed information and were unfazed by my copious note taking. Unlike the waitress the other night who got super weirded out when I took notes about the daily specials.

Not everybody got me.

Lorraine continued. "We know she missed the Full Moon meeting last night, and Deanne is trying to find out if she was at work yesterday."

"Where does Shelly work?" Jen asked, before I could, and winked at me. Warmth bloomed in my chest.

These people got me.

"She had picked up some hours cutting and repairing gemstones for that big jeweler downtown, the one with all the billboards," Lorraine replied.

"Gotcha," I nodded scribbling, *Nebraska Diamond.*

"We know, from Deanne's reporter friend that staffers from East Campus spotted a broken fence behind that old decrepit house on campus, behind the experimental cornfields." Lorraine continued.

"Where the heck is that?" Rome demanded.

"It's on that curve of Huntington at about 42nd where it turns into Leighton, north side of East Campus." Jules supplied concisely.

"Oh, yeah! Wait, does anybody live there?" Rome asked.

"No, the property belongs to the University." Lorraine gently redirected, before the chatter got off track. "A car drove into that driveway and shot straight out through the back fence and down into the creek. A woman's body has been recovered. We don't know anything yet about the ID of either the car or the body. They weren't letting reporters near the site and police are, according to Detective Rogers, not releasing the information until they have attempted to contact the victim's next of kin."

"They just found a woman's body?" I asked. "No other victims?"

Lorraine looked at me oddly. "Just a woman's body."

Nicole, her head cocked said, "So, they found a family member? But, who?" She wondered aloud.

"Detective Rogers didn't say, just that they were in another state. But she also said they couldn't release information to Charlotte, because she was a friend, not family." Lorraine said.

"Ugh," intoned Lisa, not looking up from her knitting. Nicole patted her arm, absently.

Shelly and Charlotte were best friends, not sweethearts like Nicole and Lisa. But either way, women in those sorts of *non-traditional* relationships often found themselves on the short end of the information when their friends or partners got sick or had legal issues. Not only were *friends* not considered to have the same legal rights as *family*, but in Lisa and Nicole's case, there was no way for them to become family, legally. It was terrifically frustrating.

"So, for right now," Lorraine concluded sadly. "There isn't much we can do but wait until they'll release the information."

"There's one thing!" Jen and I exclaimed at the same time.

"What's that?" Lorraine asked, stress wrinkling the corners of her eyes a touch.

I felt for her, I really did. She was facing a potentially major crisis. Loss of a Coven member impacted everyone deeply, and these were all powerfully magical women. The stakes were high. A Coven in Washington State a few years back had lost three members in a murder-suicide pact and the remaining witches turned on one another in their grief. Not only did all thirteen women die, but, well, you remember that thing with Mount St. Helen's, right?

So, yeah. Coven disruptions could be really bad news. But still, there was one piece she was definitely not picking up on and it was crucial.

Jen and I stood up and said, nearly in unison, "We have to find Tati!"

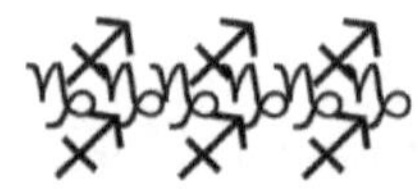

AT THE END of that long day, we did miss opening night of Predator. Jen, Jon, David and I, along with Rome, Jules, Lorraine, Nicole and Lisa, and of course, Mr. Rakow and Shadow searched the whole area between Shelly's house and the approximate accident site on East Campus where we thought she was most likely to be. Dottie stayed by the phone to wait for news.

It was long past dark with no sightings of Tati, prophetic or otherwise when beepers started to go off. Dottie was calling us home. By then the temperature had fallen slightly from its 99° high, but not much. We all piled into cars and rushed home to hear Dottie's news.

It wasn't good.

Officer Yardley stood in a solemn group with Dottie and Deanne outside the door as we arrived. He told us that the body of the woman who had crashed into Dead Man's Run on East Campus had been positively identified by photo ID and vehicle registration as Shelly.

She had lost control of her car coming around a corner and had sped through the driveway of that old abandoned house on campus. She'd crashed through the rotten old fence at the back of the property and gone down into the creek about 25 feet. She hadn't been wearing a seat belt. She died on impact with the windshield.

He said the family had been notified – a first cousin in Chicago whose name had appeared on some insurance paperwork to do with the car. He said they hadn't seen Shelly in years, but would appreciate being in contact with any local friends if plans were being made.

"I've worked with Miss Charlotte more than once at the library downtown," Office Yardley said gruffly. "She's good people. If you all could save her the heartache of finding out in the paper tomorrow, that would be a fine thing, if not strictly by-the-book."

"I caught up with him on our way out of the evening press briefing," Deanne told us. "I told him that Charlotte was Shelly's best friend, and we wanted to try to let her know as gently as possible."

Deanne was the emotional guardian of the Coven. While Lorraine tried to keep everyone practically and magically on track, Deanne looked out for everyone's well-being. She could read you in a hot minute. There was no hiding a heartbreak or a secret crush from her. Deanne knew all, and she often smoothed small disagreements long before they became big ones. She stood unobtrusively to Dottie's side, her generous curves tucked discreetly into khaki trousers and a white button down. She'd clearly stayed at work late to catch up with Officer Yardley.

Dottie wiped her eyes with a snowy white hanky and sighed deeply. She looked to Nicole and Lisa. "Ladies, I know it's been a long day and you two are hot and tired, but I have to ask you to come with us when we tell Charlotte."

"Of course," said Lisa, stepping up with Nicole's hand in hers. Both had tears silently running down their cheeks. "Of course we'll go with you."

The four of them marched sadly to their cars and headed off. Officer Yardley and Lorraine walked back to his vehicle. They spoke for a few minutes, Yardley evidently had some questions that Lorraine didn't know the answers to, based on her shrugs and baffled looks. He put away his notebook and they shook hands before he left. Rome, Jules and Mr. Rakow stood in the yard, speaking little, glumly watching Shadow destroy a bowl of water and flop, panting, in the grass.

Jen, David, Jon and I had collapsed onto the picnic table on the small concrete back patio where Dottie had left the huge sun-tea pitcher, along with a half-dozen or so *Empire Strikes Back* glasses from the Burger King collection. Bast appeared just as we returned and was now gracing the table opposite the tea pitcher. Jon started pouring and handing around glasses.

I was gross. I was coated in sweat, on top of dirt and tree debris from hunting for Tati on East Campus. Dead Man's Run, the creek where the car went into the water, flows right through the campus. It's a watershed that runs through much of town, carrying rainwater from the concrete streets away to Holmes Lake on the south side of town. University planners built around it, placing buildings strategically away from the creek and making a wide green space around it so the area adjacent to the waterway is allowed to be somewhat untamed. It wasn't as wild a space as Wilderness Park, where we still often trained, but wild enough for a layer of dirt and weeds and stickers to accumulate on me, not to mention the bug bites.

I was emotionally exhausted too. Not finding Tati, and then coming home to the worst possible news about Shelly just knocked me flat. I was almost too tired to feel sad. Almost.

Shelly had been just a really beautiful person. She had that fabulous, easy laugh and a super keen mind for the most complicated spells. She'd been with the Coven less than two years and was universally adored. Losing her was like losing fireflies from summer, or lights from the Christmas tree. Something special was missing.

There was a big ball of hurt in my chest that was going to fuel some ugly crying soon, but for the moment, my brain wouldn't let up. Bast stood, casually moved a few steps closer to me and flopped, looking pointedly at me, inviting a delicate nose stroke. I obliged.

"Guys, help me think through this. Miss Charlotte told me she lives near downtown. She walks to work whenever she can. If Shelly got into that accident on her way home from Charlotte's house, that would sort of make sense. It's on the way, and she could have been tired and overshot the curve, but" I dragged a disgustingly limp notebook out of my sweaty shorts pocket and flipped back through my notes from earlier. "When Miss Charlotte checked Shelly's house, she said she knew she'd been home first, because the garage door was open and Tati's leash was on the hook by the door."

"What are you thinking, Angie?" Jon had turned sideways on the picnic bench and stretched his legs out. His sweaty back was leaned up against my sweaty shoulder. Man, alive it was hot!

"I'm thinking," I said, wiping my forehead on the sleeve of my t-shirt, "that maybe it wasn't just an accident."

At that, Bast rose to her feet quickly and gracefully, strode across the table to Jen and very deliberately bumped Jen's forehead with her own. Jen gave me a pointed stare.

David slammed his hand down on the table. "I know you're right, Ang," he said angrily. "Yardley said she wasn't wearing her seatbelt. Shelly always wore her seatbelt. *Always.* Something doesn't add up."

I wrote *seatbelt* in my notebook without breaking David's intense gaze.

"What's getting me is, if Miss Charlotte is right and she did get home first, then to get to the spot where the car went off the road, she'd have been driving Wast, *away* from her house. Going that direction, she'd have had to turn a *really* hard left *and* go over the median to get into the driveway of that old house. That doesn't seem like a tired mistake, it seems more like a panicky or a desperate one."

"Is there some way we could tell for sure which way the car was going?" David asked. Despite the heat and our collective exhaustion, he sat up straight, perched on the outside edge of the picnic table bench, poised, as usual, for action. Jen was still staring at me, and stroking Bast expertly with one hand.

I mused. "Maybe. It's too dark right now to see anything, but I think early tomorrow morning before we meet the others to keep looking for Tati, we should go check it out. I don't know how much of the actual accident site we can look at, but for sure let's look at that median. See if we can find any clues that might not have clicked with Officer Yardley."

Bast eyed me and her purrs increased in volume.

"The earlier the better," David said. "We need to get back out looking for Tati."

I nodded. David wouldn't rest if there was an animal in trouble. Last summer when a stray cat abandoned a litter of kittens under Jen's porch, David spent weeks giving the kittens bottle feedings every two hours. And he *loved* Tati.

Then he said quietly, but savagely, "And if it wasn't an accident, then someone has a price to pay."

I thought of all the times David and Shelly had gone out walking with Tati at Wilderness after his mom died, and my heart broke a little more. I buried my face in my hands and breathed in and out deeply, trying not to just bust loose and cry.

Jen stood for a moment with her hands on David's shoulders, then she came around behind me. "Are you spending the night?" she asked, running her long nails through my tangled hair.

"Keep that up and I'll fall asleep out here," I blew out a deep breath, then sniffed and scrubbed at my eyes. "When I talked to Mom just now, she said she wanted me home tonight, given everything that's happening." I didn't say aloud that I really needed a hug from my mom, but I knew it to be so. "Walk me halfway?"

Everybody got up and we made our way down the block towards the boundary where the street light by my house met the surrounding darkness. We were just two days past the Coven's regular full moon meeting, so the waxing moon provided some light, filtering through the leaves of the trees overhead.

"What time should we get started tomorrow?" I asked, giving Jon a quick kiss goodnight.

"Early," Jen said. "Come over at eight," she said, hooking Jon's arm with her elbow and rolling her eyes at his groan over the early hour. "The whole Coven is gathering in the morning anyway. There will be no sleeping in for anyone."

"Cool," I said. "We can start at the accident site and follow the creek across campus and back to Shelly's. Hopefully Tati will be holed up near water. G'night, guys," I called softly and scooted cross the silent street back home.

A tiny movement caught the corner of my eye as I unlocked the door. I glanced quickly over my shoulder to see Bast, strolling up the driveway. I blew her a kiss. She turned gracefully and sat in a puddle of moonlight, her back to my house, keeping watch.

Mom met me at the door, fresh towels in her hand. She hugged me tightly, if briefly, and ushered me to a hot shower. "What time do you need to get up in the morning? I'll set your alarm." She gave me a peck on the forehead and disappeared with my dirty clothes. I knew when I couldn't remember how to pour shampoo that I needed to finish up fast and get some sleep. I didn't even bother to dry my hair afterwards, just collapsed into bed with it wrapped in a towel.

Saturday, June 13th, 1987

Hi 100°/Lo 66° No wind. No chance of rain.

Sun ♊ Mercury ♋ Venus ♉
on the cusp of ♊
Mars ♋ Jupiter ♈ Saturn ♐ Uranus ♑
Neptune ♑ Pluto ♏ Moon ♐

MOM MET ME the next morning at the kitchen table and I updated her on today's agenda while she fed me toast and juice. She'd already dug out my training-with-Mr.-Rakow backpack and filled it with water bottles and trail mix. She made me promise we'd take breaks.

"It's going to be another scorcher. We're set to top 100° today," she warned. I stuck my hair in a pony tail, added some bug spray and Band-aids I'd wished I had yesterday to my backpack, kissed her goodbye, and opened the oven door.

Okay, it was the front door, but my stars and striped stockings it was hot out already! Ugh. I shrugged into my backpack and trudged over to Jen's.

Jen, David and Jon sat around the kitchen table scarfing Golden Grahams and orange juice. I asked, "Has the whole Coven gotten here already?"

"Everybody except Rome and Ginny, they both had to work. And Diane had to go down to the farm in Lawrence yesterday. There was a bad storm and she went to check on the damage. She won't be back until tonight," said Jon around a mouthful of cereal and milk. If I didn't totally love the guy, that would have been super gross.

Strike that. Still gross.

"The more the merrier," I said.

"You guys ready?" David was already rinsing his bowl out in the sink. We filed out, pausing only to stick the dishes in the dishwasher and grab the car keys from the pegboard by the door.

"We'll start on the north side of the creek, mom, since you guys are starting on the south," Jen called to her mom.

Lorraine stood in the garage. The large door was open and several of the Coven members milled around, filling their travel cups with iced tea and snagging donuts from a card table. The mood was more anxious than sad. It seemed like everyone was hyper-focused on finding Tati instead of on losing Shelly. I understood, because I felt it too.

The enormity of Shelly's loss felt too big, too raw to look at square on just yet. Plus, there was nothing anyone could do until the police officially closed their investigation and released the body, so everything was sort of on hold. But Tati, well, there was something we could do about that. At least, we hoped we could.

Hope. It ignited and unified us. Jen, Jon, David and I hopped into Clint, Jen's 1971 brown Chevy Impala. Jon and I shared the enormous expanse of the back seat and Jen drove. David leaned over the seat and said, "Rakow was by the house earlier. He and Shadow are already out searching."

"Did they get any sleep at all" I wondered aloud. Mr. Rakow had insisted on, *Just one more loop* last night, after the rest of us had called it a night.

"Not much, I'd say," David replied. "Did you?" David asked. He was fidgeting in the front seat, as anxious as I'm sure Mr. Rakow was to find Tati as soon as possible.

"He wanted to go with Mr. Rakow and Shadow this morning," Jon whispered in my ear. "But Mr. Rakow told him to come with us to check out the median for tire tracks. Said he reads car evidence better than anybody."

That was true, I thought, enjoying the goosebumps I always got when Jon whispered in my ear. David had the sharpest tracking eyes of any of us, and knew way more about cars and tires. Jen pulled into the parking lot of the apartment complex across the street from the driveway where Shelly had gone off the road. We were approaching from the direction she'd have been driving *if* Charlotte was right and she'd gone home first, then taken off again for some reason.

The road curved right, or north first, following the curve of the creek, before bearing slightly left to straighten out again. To make the turn from this angle, she'd have probably had to swing wide right and then slam the wheel around to the left, going over the median which was raised up a good four or five inches and was dotted with ornamental trees, crossing two lanes of on-coming traffic, and nailing a dark driveway shrouded in trees. The odds against doing it accidentally seemed astro-nomically hinky. Maybe there was some other explanation for the open garage door and Tati's leash.

Evidence, I told myself. *Follow the evidence.*

"If she made that turn, even at the posted speed limit, she'd have left marks," David predicted. We piled out of the car David darted across the first two lanes be-fore I was even out of the back seat. We watched as he strode up and down the median, peering first at the on-coming lanes, then the grassy divider, then the driveway across the street.

"See anything?" Jon called. "Need a second set of eyes?"

"Yeah, man. Take a look at this and tell me what you think," David called.

Jon closed his eyes. It wasn't super obvious when he *jumped* into David to see through his eyes, I only knew exactly when he left his body when he snagged me with one pinky. We'd learned that his body operated somewhat less gracefully when he wasn't *driving* it.

Mr. Rakow and David had driven that lesson home one unforgettable afternoon during a water balloon fight in the yard. Mr. Rakow wanted to make the point that if we were up against anything more lethal than water balloons, Jon's body was very nearly a sitting duck when he was *hitchhiking* on one of us and we needed to factor that into our defenses. So, when Jon hooked my pinky with his, I grabbed his arm and slung it over my shoulder in case we needed to maneuver from our current position on the sidewalk.

Jen waited for a break in the sparse Saturday morning traffic and dashed across to join David in the median.

"What do you see?" I called.

"Tire marks, but lots of them," David called back.

There was a wide quiet break in traffic just then, so tugged on Jon's arm and we stepped quickly across the street.

"Some old, some newer," Jon said thoughtfully. "Nothing definitive."

"Well, crap." I groused. "I was really hoping for something big and obvious."

"Yeah," Jon concurred. "But it would explain why the police didn't mention it, I guess. Jen," he asked his twin, "Are you getting anything?"

Jen knelt among the plants and road debris, her hands out – searching. Her eyes closed. "Nothing yet…" and she froze, and then violently flinched.

David had snagged her by the beltloop the second she froze. The median in between four lanes of traffic was really not the place to have a prophecy-related mishap. When she flinched, he caught her in the circle of his arms.

"Speak, Prophet." His command and her response were nearly drowned out by a garbage truck in the inside lane. The driver craned back to look at us and very nearly crossed the median himself.

Crap!

"Come on!" David hollered. He grabbed Jen's hand and sprinted across the remaining two lanes of traffic to the secluded driveway where Shelly's car had gone, dragging her along. Jon returned to his own driver's seat and he and I followed them, crossing the street most ricky-tick, as Mr. Rakow would say.

"What did you find?" I demanded breathlessly.

Jen opened her hand and held out a tiny nugget that glowed golden brown in the morning sunlight. I peered at it closely without touching.

That's amber!" I exclaimed. Jen winked at me, the *just-got-rushed-by-a-herd-of-buffalo* feeling that sometimes accompanied a prophecy evidently starting to wear off.

"What's more," Jon said, his eyes closed again, this time *seeing* with his twin's eyes, and with his own magical ability, "This chunk of prehistoric tree goop was blessed by Mom's Coven!" His voice had an awestruck edge to it.

"What is it? How can you tell that? What can you see?" I asked, excitedly.

Jon reached his arms out to me and David on his other side, inviting our touch. He often did this to share a snapshot of what something looked like the way he could perceive things now. It was freaky fascinating.

We caught hold of his hands and as one, stared at the

tiny, pea-gravel sized piece of amber, and gasped.

A tiny light show danced all around it in an intricate, thirteen-sided geometric pattern. A *tridecagram*, according to my geometry textbook. One look at the colors and patterns of this one and it was clear as day to me it had been touched by Lorraine's Coven.

I stared, fascinated at the tiny three-dimensional light show as it encircled the tiny piece of amber like a protective atmosphere that thrummed with its own heartbeat. Furthermore, each of the thirteen lines and points bore the elemental signature of the witch who had cast it.

Lorraine's strong, straight silvery purple energy marked her line and point. Lisa's line was the gold color of wheat under August sunshine, and Nicole's line right next to Lisa's was a deep, marine blue. Dorothy's line was a pure and shining silver, as strong as Lorraine's but with a depth Lorraine's did not *yet?* possess. Shelly's deep rose red line seemed undiminished by her death, another curiosity for me to obsessively ponder later.

Diane's line was a deep forest green, and Jules' line the color of sun-blasted sand. Rome's brilliant fuchsia line balanced against Deanne's neighboring sky blue. Both Becky's and Elizabeth's lines were of such deep purple and blue to rival blackness, while Pat's line contained points of both deep true black and pale feathery grey within it. Ginny's, the thirteenth line was the brilliant new green of spring shoots burdened with life.

From this, Jon's perspective, I could see that the tiny piece of amber didn't sit on Jen's hand, but floated millimeters above it, buoyed and protected by the magic.

"Whoa!" was David's appreciative response.

"Holy metaphysical geometry, Batman" I said. "That is so freaking cool! And it's a clue for sure, but I know they lay blessings on lots of stuff that they sell at the garage sales. Can we know for sure that this piece is from Shelly on Wednesday night?"

"Unfortunately, yes." Jen replied, closing her fist around the pebble. "That's where the vision comes in. In it, I was in the car with Shelly as she went out of control and crossed the road. She wasn't alone in the car." Jen said. Her voice sounded tight.

"Could you see? Could you see who it was?" David demanded, bouncing on the tips of his toes, his fists clenched.

"I couldn't." Jen swallowed and looked uncomfortable. Jen rarely betrayed her emotions, so something must have really gotten to her about this vision. I lay my hand on her back and felt her take a shuddery breath.

"Because I was seeing from that other person's eyes. I was attacking Shelly and driving her off the road." She looked at us, her eyes wide and troubled. "It was horrible, and vicious." She turned her head and spat, like she had a bad taste in her mouth.

David put his arm around Jen on her other side and he and Jon did the forearm grip thing they did on account of being too manly to hold hands. Jen's, David's and my necklaces glowed comfortably and I could feel Jon, *hitch-hiking* over my shoulder, separately bonded to each of us. We stayed that way, the four of us on the sidewalk in front of the abandoned house where our friend had died, and we gathered our strength.

"We've got to figure out who did this." I said firmly.

"We do," David agreed. "But first, we have to find Tati!"

Jenny tucked the piece of amber into the watch pocket of her cutoffs. We separated with an abbreviated high-five routine and proceeded down the driveway toward the abandoned house. John's grip on my hand tightened.

"What's up?" I asked.

"This is a weird place," he said vaguely. I looked at him quizzically. "Nothing that feels or looks like Shelly or the car, but yeah. Lots of hinky stuff here, or about to be here?"

Back then, that property was in some sort of real estate limbo. The University was in the process of buying it, but the deal got soured several times before they got it. Once they did, they turned it into a lab for their forensic science students. The thing Jon sensed that was *about to be here* turned out to be a scientific boneyard where decay was studied in order to solve crimes. CSI Lincoln, NE.

Ew.

A tiny scuffling sound reached my ear. I looked fast. Whatever was escaping away into the bushes disappeared with a rustle of leaves and a flash of black. I shivered.

"Let's get moving. Is there any decent place to cross the creek?" I called to Jen and David who were already through the hole Shelly's car had made in the fence and wading through the weeds. The tow truck had left deep tracks where it had parked to pull the car out, and a bunch of weeds were trampled all around, but things were already starting to bounce back. Mother Nature didn't screw around. She got busy with the business of living pdq.

"It's been so dry," Jon mused, picking his way carefully with my guidance. "There should be a low spot someplace."

We found a spot, and within minutes we were on the south side of Dead Man's Run where the campus looked more like a traditional college, and less like a freaky horror movie set. It wasn't even 8:30 a.m. and I was already drenched in sweat.

We made our way across campus, calling Tati between sips from our water bottles. Lorraine and her group were starting to our west, in amongst the campus buildings, thinking Tati was maybe looking for humans. They'd planned out a grid and copied "LOST DOG" signs with pictures of Tati's cute face on them to tack up or hand out. Mr. Rakow and Shadow were working their way through the fenced off experimental fields, specially chaperoned by one of the campus groundskeepers who happened to be an old Army buddy of his.

By 10:00, we had looped and swirled all around Dead Man's Run as it meandered through campus, and were all the way to 48th Street, the east boundary of campus. We checked in with Mr. Rakow at our pre-arranged spot, and were instructed to continue east past the swimming pool and the park towards Shelly's house. They were going to loop back around one final field and then they'd meet us there.

After Dead Man's Run exited campus, it ran underneath 48th St., reemerging in the park where it bisected the picnic area from the swimming pool. The area around the fence where the rising sunlight had decimated Mitch, the undead jerkface now sported a patch of wildflowers that bloomed defiantly no matter how much the Park's groundskeepers neglected them or mowed over them.

Mr. Rakow was pretty sure if Tati was scared, she'd go to ground near the creek. It ran right behind Shelly's house and Tati intimately knew every blade of grass in this park. She'd feel safe around here, or so we hoped.

We emerged from the weeds up onto the bridge just across from Shelly's house. Several of the Coven members must already be there, judging from the familiar cars parked on the street.

"Here come Mr. Rakow and Shadow," said David,

peering back the way we'd come through the park. I caught the movement of Mr. Rakow's camouflage bucket-hat bobbing through the tall weeds on the side of the creek. Shadow bounded down the steep bank and into the creek with a quiet splash. He inspected something along the edge of the waterline, then turned and bounded back up the bank, spraying water from his shaggy black and brown fur.

"Still looking, I guess," I murmured sadly.

We trudged across the wide street bridge towards Francis St. Shelly's was the second house from the corner. A breeze lifted the sweaty hair on my neck that had escaped my pony tail, but it was a hot breeze from the south.

"Ugh," I said.

"What's that smell? Is somebody out barbequing in this heat?" Jen asked then she exclaimed, "Hey! Look at the driveway."

We looked. Both the gravel driveway and the walkway from the drive to the front stoop had been liberally sprinkled with tiny pieces of amber, identical to the one we'd found in the median.

A car pulled over to the curb just ahead of us and the driver climbed out. She moved slowly and deliberately as though she was having to consciously convince her limbs to respond.

"Miss Charlotte!" I took a couple of running steps towards her, my arms outstretched. I stopped when she looked at me.

I'd known Miss Charlotte for years now, and had benefited from her research help many times. She was, under ordinary circumstances, one of the most cheerful and chatty people I knew. Her brown eyes sparkled when she told stories about her cat, Smokey, about new mysteries she was reading, and of course about whatever I was researching. She wasn't just a font; she was an enthusiastically bubbling fountain of wonderfully sharable information.

Today was different. Her usual summer uniform of jeans and a library Summer Reading Program t-shirt looked wrinkled and slept in. Her energy was stilled. She was motionless like a lone oarsman in a life raft. Her shocked aloneness was palpable. She looked at me and smiled the saddest of smiles.

Jen crowded me into her and enfolded us both in the embrace of her long arms. The boys stood silently close by. Our necklaces glowed warmly as we circled around her. The chatter from the nearby Coven members stilled and the moment thrummed slowly like a heartbeat.

A heartbeat which was shockingly interrupted by barking! I recognized Shadow's happy bark at once. We jumped, en masse, and sprinted across the amber speckled driveway to the far side of Shelly's house. David got to the heavy gate first and wrestled it open, rushing down the backyard while the rest of us crowded through in an ungainly knot.

Emerging from the creek where it ran behind Shelly's house, muddy and triumphant, three figures climbed up the bank. Mr. Rakow's fist shot up in the air, a gesture of both greeting and success. Shadow leapt out of the tall weeds, his tail wagging his whole body. Between them scurried Tati!

Her beautiful golden fur was filthy with mud and leaves. She moved excitedly but fearfully, head down, tail wagging ferociously but still tucked between her legs. Poor thing was a wreck! I wondered if she'd slept at all since the early morning hours of Thursday.

David reached them first. Once Tati spotted him, she

nearly went airborne. She tackled him to the grass and they rolled around, a dirty happy wagging crying mess.

"She's found! Blessed Goddess she's found!" Ginny cried, her curly shock of red hair glowing like fire in the blazing sunshine. David dug treats out of his pockets, and Tati devoured them while Shadow sat protectively, and not just a little proudly nearby, and everyone crowded around.

Elizabeth and Becky, the two youngest witches in the Coven tried to direct the group, reminding them that Tati was probably super freaked out. "We don't want to spook her and send her running again." Becky warned the others in a low, quiet voice.

"Who has a leash?" called Elizabeth quietly over her shoulder.

"I do," said Charlotte, approaching at a measured pace. She drew up even with David and knelt, the leash slung over her shoulder, tears running unchecked down her cheeks. Tati scrambled over David's leg, and hurled herself headlong into Charlotte's arms.

As soon as Tati's leash was secured, the Coven's quiet, tearful murmurs erupted into a happy, excited buzz of conversation.

"Where was she?"

"Where did you find her?"

"Is she hurt?"

"Is she okay?" The questions tumbled over one another. Mr. Rakow grinned.

"She was just on this side of the bridge!" Mr. Rakow pointed. "Not even a hundred meters from the house. She's fine! No breaks or bleeds, some heat exhaustion probably. We should probably get her up to the house where she can cool off and have some fresh water."

"Why would she have stayed out there?" wondered

Deanne aloud. "She has a dog house in the yard, she could at least have taken shelter. Why wouldn't she have come up into the yard?"

"You've been leaving food and water by the dog house, haven't you?" Nicole asked Charlotte.

"I have, and it hadn't been touched," Charlotte said confused but laughing, her arms and lap full of a squirmy, dirty, happy Tati.

"I wonder," Jon mused quietly in my ear.

"That sweet girl needs a meal, a nap and a bath, in that order!" Lorraine said firmly, ushering everyone up out of the yard.

Everyone obeyed, each joyfully taking a moment for rubs on Tati's head and hugs for Charlotte. Their chatter was a low, excited hum punctuated by happy exclamations and laughter.

"What do you wonder?" I asked Jon quietly.

"I wonder what she was avoiding," he replied.

"Up at the house? You think something is scaring her, something that's still hanging around?" I asked squinting up at the house.

It was just past noon. The house and yard were well shaded by big oaks. The creek, on the other hand, was exposed to the blazing sun. Mr. Rakow had said she was by the bridge, I suppose there would be a little shade there, but Deanne was right. Why hide out under a bridge, when you have ready access to your dog house, food, water, and shade?

I looked around from this vantage point. Shelly's back yard was fenced, mostly. The aging weathered privacy fence that divided her from her neighbors on each side was in pretty good shape, but along the back of the property line where it abutted Dead Man's Run, the ground was uneven and subject to the whims of the creek bed's shifting. Several of the fenceposts had leaned sharply, allowing the rails to collapse and leaving wide gaps like the one where Mr. Rakow and the dogs had entered the yard from the creek side.

That's when I noticed some new fence posts leaning against the fence up by the house. It looked like fence repairs had already been set in motion.

Shadow had navigated through the group of humans, receiving his due of, *Good Dog*s and ear skritches for his role in Tati's rescue. Once that important detail had been attended to, Shadow was free to run the perimeter, one of his regular duties.

I watched the Coven trudge back up the incline of Shelly's backyard, toward the gate we'd come in by. Jules and Rome, deep in conversation were out front, the rest of the Coven spread out behind them like individual wildflowers making up an unconventional bouquet.

Each witch had some unique element that separated them from the usual, sedately uninteresting grownups of the rest of my world. Individually each woman was pretty great, but together, even non-magically like this, just gathered outdoors midday, they shone with a combined essence that I could sense without even asking Jon to let me "see."

Shadow had worked his way along the back and side of the fence and seemed pretty interested in something on the northwest side of the house, near those fenceposts I'd noticed. There wasn't a gate on that side. You had to go through the currently closed, people-sized door at the back of the garage Shadow started whining urgently which attracted Mr. Rakow's immediate attention

I watched Mr. Rakow sharply turn and jog diagonally across the yard toward Shadow who was becoming increasingly agitated.

"Let's go," David said, striding past. Jen snagged Jon's other arm and we followed apace. Shadow's hindquarters were vibrating. He didn't want to wait. He wanted to jump the six-foot fence and GO. He gave an excited glance back over his shoulder at Mr. Rakow, who made the call.

"Okay!" Mr. Rakow's command cut sharply through the various conversations happening and everyone turned to look. Tati cowered in Miss Charlotte's arms.

Shadow leapt over the fence from his standing position like it was just an everyday effort. He touched the top of the fence with one paw, deliberately re-angling his landing on the back side. We heard a frenzied scrabbling, digging sound. David and Mr. Rakow reached the garage door just as Shadow's explosive barking began. Jon, Jen and I were only steps behind.

Shelly's garage had three people-sized doors; the one we'd just come through from the backyard, the one that led into the kitchen, and the one that led out to the small strip of yard on the northwest side of the house. Mr. Rakow and David had thrown the door wide open, and through it I could see a strip of weedy gravel about three feet wide that ran the length of the garage. It was deeply shaded by the tall hedge that acted as a privacy break between her house and the neighbors who lived on the corner.

Back here, Shelly had stacked the rest of the wood for the fence repair project, along with a few other bulky items that didn't fit nicely in the garage – some grill parts, and a broken porch swing.

Shadow was whining and barking, urgently pawing at the pile of fence rails. Jen and I crowded into the doorway with Jon behind us, *looking* over our shoulders physically and metaphysically.

David and Mr. Rakow were pulling rails off the pile. Underneath was a heavy plastic tarp concealing a dark lump. I smelled charcoal, and then Shadow tugged at a corner of the tarp and the smell really hit us.

Oh, man. That smell.

Mr. Rakow looked up. "Someone go call the non-emergency number, see if you can get Yardley or Officer Rogers over here right away."

Jen, who had the most sensitive nose, jogged off to find the phone. David darted through the doorway and out front, taking deep, deliberate breaths of fresh air. I pulled back, but then peeked around the corner of the doorway, holding my nose against the pervading odor of decomposition. Mr. Rakow had pulled the tarp off the dead man's face, and I stared at it, fascinated.

It was bad, but by then, I'd seen worse. The blood from his belly wound had mostly soaked into the bare dry ground underneath him, so there wasn't a pool or anything. The part of his face that wasn't bashed in was a mass of shallow scratches. I was sure I didn't recognize him. I probably wouldn't have been quite as sure just based on looking at his face, but this guy had a very distinctive black pompadour. He almost looked like an Elvis impersonator or something. I was sure I'd have noticed that if I'd seen this dude before.

Whoever had concealed the body had first dumped on it the contents of the large, now empty bag of charcoal that had been crammed haphazardly under the hedge. Tucked around that and the body was a heavy sheet of outdoor tarp, the green kind with grommets that you could tie over porch furniture in the winter. The fence boards were piled on top.

But it was hot out. Really hot. I squinted against the tears flowing from my eyes. Lorraine pulled me and Jon back from the door with one hand, her other hand pinching her nose shut.

"Get out of there, you guys. Officer Yardley is on his way and they'll want to see everything undisturbed. You know how methodical he is. Besides, that smell is hideous." She gave us a gentle shove toward the kitchen door. "Go inside and cool off."

Behind her came Charlotte and Dottie. Laura and Nicole had taken Tati inside and Dottie had her arms around Miss Charlotte's shoulders. They both looked quite upset. Lorraine took Charlotte's hand and looked carefully at her.

"Can you stand to look?" she asked.

"Yes. I want to see who it is," Charlotte's voice was tight with stress.

"Okay, go ahead and look." Dottie stepped through the door with Charlotte. Mr. Rakow again lifted the tarp away from the dead man's face.

"Do you know him?" Lorraine asked.

"I sure do," Charlotte replied, clinching her fists and spitting out the words. Dottie folded her lips tightly shut. "His name is Viktor. He's Shelly's ex-boyfriend from Ohio. He's been stalking her for years."

"What?" Lorraine exclaimed. "How did I know nothing about this? Did anybody else know that Shelly had an ex who was bothering her?"

She stared around at the witches who were all now crowding around the kitchen door and window, out of the way, but hanging on every word. A murmur of surprised, *no's* went around the group.

"Why wouldn't she have asked for the Coven's help?" Lorrain asked, sadness and confusion crowding her expression. "Maybe we could have…"

Dottie turned suddenly from Charlotte and placed a

hand on Lorraine's arm. "Stop!" she insisted. "Don't start blaming yourself for any of this. If Shelly didn't tell us, she may have had her reasons."

Officer Yardley pulled swiftly but safely into the driveway in his patrol car. No lights, no sirens. He spoke into his radio mic briefly, giving his position and then stepped out of his car and approached. Officer Yardley was not a super imposing looking guy. He was of average height and build, probably somewhere between 40 and 50 years old. I'm honestly not sure if I'd have recognized him without his uniform.

His vibe, however, was quite different. When Officer Yardley walked on to a scene, everybody relaxed a little bit. He carried with him a sense of compassionate order, sort of like that really cool camp counselor or lifeguard who'd been there the longest and knew all the ropes. The ones everybody looked to when the tornado sirens went off or some dumb kid choked on a hot dog. He always knew just what to say and do, and folks felt it. When he entered the garage, he was met by the palpable goodwill of the Coven.

I thought for the briefest flicker of a moment how dreadful it would be if these two powerful forces, the Police and the Coven, were not allied, and I shuddered.

"Afternoon, Lorraine, Rakow, Miss Charlotte. If you'll all just take a step back and let me have a look see?" He stepped through the door, nodded to Mr. Rakow who came back through and closed the door behind him.

"He wants statements from everybody, but he has help coming so it won't take forever. Of course, he'll want to talk to you first, Miss Charlotte."

"Of course," she said fiercely. "I have a few choice things to tell him about Viktor," she continued through clenched teeth.

I personally was dying to hear all about Viktor. Stalking wasn't anything I really understood too well. It wasn't until a couple of years later when an actress from a popular sitcom was murdered by her stalker in California that people started enacting laws about it. In 1987 there weren't any laws on the books in Lincoln defining stalking or harassment and elevating them to criminal status. Not until the 1990's.

I knew, in a vague way that sometimes women got legal protection orders against abusive exes, but those were mostly in the news when they got broken. So, if this guy had been stalking Shelly, there wouldn't have been much done about it. As to why she hadn't involved the Coven? That I'd be interested to discover.

Lorraine came over from the front porch where she'd been talking to Dottie and put her hand on David's shoulder. "Once Officer Yardley has talked to Charlotte, I'd like him to speak with you and Rakow next so you can take the dogs home. Tati needs a good looking over, and a bath.

David and Mr. Rakow agreed happily, as much to be *doing* something rather than standing around waiting as to take care of Tati. As the afternoon wore on, I had reason to be jealous of their early dismissal.

It was nearly suppertime before Officer Yardley and Officer Rogers finally finished up with the Coven, and with removal of the body. Folks had filtered out as they were excused, the plan was to meet back up at Lorraine's, order pizza and discuss what to do next.

Jen and I got a ride back over to Clint the Impala with Deanne, and I had Jen drop me at home so I could update my folks on the events of the afternoon.

After I'd answered all their thousand questions about the dead guy and Tati, I ducked into my room to pack my backpack for my originally planned overnight at Jen's.

"Everyone is getting together at Lorraine's tonight to decide if there's any spellcraft they can work that might help untangle the details around this mess and figure out what really happened to Shelly." I said to my mom who was leaning in my bedroom doorway, a dishtowel thrown over one shoulder. "Oh, and Lorraine said to tell you pizza is being delivered at 7:30, and you guys are welcome if you want to come."

"Share our thanks, but we already have supper going so we'll touch base with her later and Charlotte later. How is Charlotte doing, by the way?"

"She's awfully broken up," I replied somberly. "She and Shelly were, like, the absolute best of friends."

Mom sighed. "Yeah, I ran into them at a library program last summer they both have … *had* … such bubbly personalities. It was a great time. What a tragedy."

"You and dad knew Shelly's mom too, didn't you?" I asked, cramming a few more things into my already stuffed backpack.

"We did! She was a dear friend of Dottie's. I don't know if you were even old enough to remember, but when Dottie was still teaching at Wesleyan, she and Shelly's mom, Janet, would come for dinner sometimes."

"I don't remember that!" I exclaimed. "But then Dottie's been retired for quite a while now."

"Yes, I think it's been close to fifteen years, now. I'm not surprised you don't remember it."

"Did Shelly come over too? With her mom and Dottie?" I asked.

"No, she was already away at school by then. Let's see, in Chicago, right hon?" She leaned back and addressed my dad who had settled in his easy chair with the paper. He lowered it across his lap and cocked his head, thinking.

"Chicago, yes, but not the U. Wasn't she at Northwestern for her undergrad?" Dad asked.

"Yes! That's it. Then she did her post-grad at the Art Institute, right in Chicago. I remember she was in town when Mayor Daley passed," Mom recalled.

"1973," Dad mused

"I'll see you guys tomorrow," I said, shrugging my backpack over my shoulder and pausing in my bedroom doorway for a hug from Mom.

"Will you be home for lunch tomorrow?" Mom asked. I'm frying chicken," she said temptingly.

"I'm totally in!" I said, hugging her hard. I kissed dad's head on my way past and zoomed out the door, nearly mowing Mallory down as she came through the door.

"Hey weirdo," she greeted me.

"Hey lameo," I responded.

Mallory paused in the doorway, blocking me. "There's a stray cat hanging around, have you seen it?" she asked.

"No, I don't think so. Why?" I asked.

"Bast doesn't like it," she replied.

"What do you mean?" I asked. Bast rarely bothered herself with other cats, beyond the usual supercilious stare.

"I saw her, just now. She chased it up the elm tree on the corner." She shrugged and pointed out the tree with her housekey. "Look. She's still there, guarding the tree. Weird." Mallory pushed past me and went inside.

I looked to the tree she'd pointed out, and sure enough, Bast was sitting in a pose of elegant ferocity and looking steadily upwards. I crossed the street and approached her.

"Hey beautiful, what's cookin'?" I craned my neck, looking up into the tree, trying to see what bast was looking at, but I couldn't see much beyond a flash of black fur, mostly concealed on a leafy branch. I reached down and scratched Bast's head exactly where she liked it. She turned from her intense gaze at the tree for just long enough to butt sweetly at my hand, and then returned her laser focus on the tree.

I shrugged and moved on down the sidewalk. It was after 5:00 and still stupidly hot. I shifted my backpack. I'd been outside all of three minutes and my sweaty everything was stuck to my sweaty everything else.

Barf.

By the time I got over to Jen and Jon's, nearly all the Coven had gathered. The only cars I didn't see were Lorraine's and Dottie's. I stuck my head in the kitchen door and Jen snagged me by the shirt sleeve and hauled me inside.

"Go toss your stuff on my bed and come help me squeeze lemons," she directed.

"Oooh, homemade lemonade?" I cooed. That was a treat.

"Dottie was in Petaluma last week," Jen called after me as I jogged through the living room to the bedroom. "Her kids sent her home with a bushel basket full of Meyer lemons from their tree!"

I tossed my backpack on the bed and watched it wave up and down. Jen had a waterbed. I wasn't always a huge fan, but during the summer, no matter how hot it was outside, I always slept like a baby on those cool waves. I was looking forward to it tonight, for sure.

I scurried back into the kitchen. Deanne sat at the kitchen table with Nicole and Lisa constructing a salad, or a soup, or possibly a spell, sometimes it was hard to tell.

But the elegantly sliced carrots and bell peppers pushed the odds towards salad, in my view.

"What do you need done first?" I asked Jen who was stirring a giant glass jar of lemons and ice. She ladled me a teacup full.

"Does it have enough sugar?" She laughed when I crossed my eyes and scooped in another half a cupful.

"Start making a space big enough in the fridge to fit this behemoth, plus that blue salad bowl, would you please?" Jen asked, turning back to her concoction.

"What did Officer Yardley ask you, Angie?" asked Deanne. She looked at me a little desperately. Deanne wasn't into food prep like Lisa and Nicole were. She looked like she'd love a reason to take a break. I settled down in front of the open fridge door and started rearranging.

"He asked me to walk him through everything we'd done since that morning, where we found Tati, and finding the body. What did Miss Charlotte say the dude's name was? Viktor? So, who is he, or was he exactly?"

"He was Shelly's ex," Nicole offered, her long, elegantly beringed fingers seeming to hardly touch the peppers she was slicing. They seemed to simply dance briefly with her knife and then leap gracefully off to the side of her cutting board, perfectly portioned.

"They were never married, Charlotte said, but they were engaged for six months," she went on. I swear, the air around her hands shimmered happily, like it was just giddy to be near her.

"Where did they meet?" Deanne asked, sneaking a pepper slice and poking a tiny knife at the carrot she was supposed to be chopping.

"In college. They were in undergrad together for most of a year, anyway. She said he was kind of rudderless, would show up for the first week or so of class then just fade away. He was in danger of failing out, but avoided it by getting into a fist fight with one of his professors and getting himself expelled, instead."

"Oh, wow," said Lisa. She appeared torn between artfully arranging the greens in a huge blue stoneware bowl and whatever was calling her name from the knitting bag in the empty chair next to her.

"He floated around, Charlotte told me, had various jobs, sometimes in a band. He was a talented singer and pianist, she said, but could never hang on to a gig for long. He's either blow off shows or get into fights and get kicked out." Nicole shook her head and poked cherry tomatoes into place with long fingernails painted midnight blue.

"And Shelly put up with all that?" Deanne asked, amazed.

"She did, for a long time," Nicole replied. "It was all terribly dramatic. She was head over heels for him. They fought and broke up dozens of times, and she'd take him back. Charlotte said Shelly was in way over her head. Then when she decided to go to grad school instead of going along with his half-baked plan to hitchhike across Europe, the engagement imploded."

"So, then what happened?" I asked from my spot on the floor, half in and half out of the fridge. "Did she take him back again?"

"Charlotte said it was a near thing. He came to her place in town after she'd been working on her Masters for a year. They started off all gung-ho, but then Viktor disappeared for two days on a drinking binge and when he turned back up, they fought. He trashed her apartment. That's when he started calling all the time, and following her, and waiting for her on campus. At one point, he made a scene with her graduate advisor, and the police got involved. He'd lay off for a while, she'd think he had finally given up on her for good, and then he'd start up again."

"This has been going on for years?" I asked, appalled. "And the police never stopped it?"

Nicole sighed heavily Lisa shook her head. "It's complicated," Nicole said sadly.

I didn't quite know what to do with that. In a lot of ways, I was still blissfully naïve. Even after the last several years we'd spent fighting monsters, I'd lucked out with a great dad and a great boyfriend. I knew that not every guy was a prince, but back then, I still believed in love, and good guys.

"When she moved back here to take care of her mom, she really thought she'd lost him, but he turned up like a bad penny," Nicole said.

"How did he find her?" I asked. In 1987, the world wide web was still a gleam in Tim Berners-Lee's eye. He was at CERN, but his groundbreaking combination of hypertext, TCP and DNS didn't get proposed until 1989. All that is to say, finding someone who didn't want to be found was more difficult in 1987 than any time since.

I didn't get my question answered just then on account of the yelling and the explosion in the garage.

Jen thrust the big lemonade jar into my hands and straight-armed the screen door open. She was halfway to the garage before I got the jar in, my butt off the floor and the fridge door slammed shut. Deanne, Nicole and Lisa rushed through right behind me.

When Jen threw the garage door open, a shower fuchsia and leaf green sparks burst out.

The five of us tumbled through the door like something out of a *Three Stooges* routine. I barely kept my feet.

The witches were in the process of setting up the garage for a Coven meeting. The giant candle-bearing chandelier had been lowered from the rafters and was sitting on a card table in the center of the garage.

Rome, Ginny, Elizabeth and Becky had been tasked with set-up detail. The usual tables had been lined up in the corners, leaving the four cardinal directions clear. Those tables were draped in velvet cloths and ritual items had been placed out, mostly in wicker baskets set along long macrame table runners, because that's how Lorraine rolled.

Once the meeting began, the chandelier would be raised up and the table beneath it removed, leaving the large center space free for the coven to sit or stand or dance or whatever was required of the activity they had planned.

They had already unrolled the huge old Persian rug that covered the concrete floor. Most of the chairs were stacked or hung, but two had been hastily pulled out in one corner and there sat Elizabeth and Becky, raptly staring at the other two and sharing a box of Milk Duds like they were at the movies.

At the center table, one on either side of the chandelier stood Rome and Ginny glaring at one another, neither seeming to notice the magical sparks that were literally cascading off of them while they argued.

"That is so like you to try defend him!" Rome yelled.

"Of course it is!" Ginny yelled right back. "He's my boyfriend, why wouldn't I?"

Rome towered over Ginny, who barely topped five feet. Whenever the witches made reference to 'the goddess,' Rome was always the figure in my mind. She was everything most women were, but taller and stronger and brighter and louder. Much louder. Right now, her fingertip length white blonde hair stood straight up and gave the effect of a glowing crown. She held a cream-colored candle in each hand and the warmth of her hands was starting to make the wax melt. I could smell the lavender and lemon verbena Lorraine had used to make them.

Ginny, albeit tiny, was no slouch. On the contrary, she faced Rome from a position of equal power. She glared at Rome like an angry red-maned lion.

"Guys!" Jen started and was utterly ignored.

"Ginny, Chuck is an ass! He comes into the diner all the time and flirts with anything in a skirt! In the mornings he's pissed off and hung over, and if he comes in for supper with that pack of half-witted friends of his, they're all already half in the bag by six o'clock and raising hell!" Rome raged.

"He is good to me!" Ginny retorted.

Rome rolled her eyes and yelled, "He's a player and a red-neck jerk! Jimmy spotted him in the hall by the bathrooms last week, he had a girl pinned to the wall. Jimmy had to haul him off of her. He had to threaten to call the cops before Chuck would leave. And every time he comes in, no matter how hot it is outside, you know he leaves those dogs in his truck!"

"Chuck is a licensed breeder! He'd never endanger any of the dogs!" Ginny spat.

"Ha!" Rome exploded. "Chuck is not selling those dogs to hunters, he is selling them to dog fighters, Ginny!" Rome yelled. Fuchsia sparks exploded all around her. "Why are you still with him? You deserve so much better!"

The five of us had silently edged around the garage until we drew close to Elizabeth and Becky.

"What the heck?" I hissed.

"Ginny's boyfriend is a jerk, and everybody knows it but Ginny. He's a regular at Rome's diner, and as soon as she realized this was the guy Ginny's been seeing, she went off!" Becky whispered, offering me a Milk Dud.

"Yeah?" I asked. We all flinched as another round of sparks fountained from the center of the room. I felt cold. The old AC seemed to be set on *nuclear freeze* setting.

I'd have given my left arm for a month in a lab with super smart people figuring out exactly how magical energy worked, but back then all I knew was that it worked, and for the purposes of our extra-curricular otherworldly activities, I just had to trust that. I filed it away under *future goals* and refocused on Becky.

Becky was the youngest member of the Coven, at nineteen. She'd graduated high school the year after Elizabeth and had tried to make a living playing gigs with her punk band, Skurge Puppies. Eventually, her mom kicked her out of their apartment an she couch-surfed for about a year before Dottie caught her at the mall, using magic to shoplift.

Dottie and Lorraine decided it was safest for everyone if Becky could be taken off the streets and taught magic properly before she hurt herself or someone else by accident.

It was my general understanding that anybody could use magic to a certain degree, but some people were just better at it than others. Becky was one of those that was really good at it. I'd wondered before if there was a musical correlation to magical talent, but my pool of examples was woefully small, scientifically speaking.

"Yeah," she went on, tucking a strand of long brown hair behind an ear that was pierced from top to bottom. "I know the guy from around. He's trouble. Like, big money and gambling and selling illicit stuff, not just those fighting dogs. But I guess he's heavenly on the eyes and in the sack, so he's got no problem finding girlfriends, and he digs redheads."

"For the love of the goddess, Ginny, Chuck is no good! And you know it, too! That's what I can't figure out…" Suddenly Rome cocked her head and peered at Ginny. "Oh, Ginny, honey." Rome's voice dropped several decibels and gained warmth. "What's wrong?"

For a moment, I thought Ginny was going to explode. The tension was rolling off of her in palpable waves and her eyes were wild.

Rome reached out a hand, palm up, and Ginny sort of melted, like she'd been doused with rainwater. Ginny's breath hitched once, twice before she whispered, "I'm pregnant."

Instantly the other five witches were on their feet, encircling Ginny in their arms, the rattle of conversation rocketing from shock to dismay to joy and protestations of support.

"You just move right in with us!"

"Nobody would ever find the body, I swear."

Jen took my hand and we made our way past the women and out of the garage. We were still a few paces from the door when it swung open, slowly. Lorraine entered, looking troubled.

"What happened, Mom?" Jen asked, rushing to her, arms out.

Lorraine gathered her tall daughter under one arm and me under the other and kissed both of us on top of the head before taking a deep breath and facing the assembled.

"The police have detained Charlotte for additional questioning. Officer Yardley says she'll have to spend the night in jail," she reported dully.

"What?" Rome roared.

"Why?" Nicole cried out.

"What do they think happened?" Lisa demanded.

"Yardley doesn't think it, but his supervisor thinks Charlotte killed Viktor to protect Shelly, then she and Shelly argued, and Shelly drove off upset, or maybe Charlotte was chasing her and caused the car accident. He said they don't have enough evidence right now for an arrest, but they can hold her for questioning for even a day or two before they have to make an official arrest!" Lorraine sounded exhausted.

"She needs an attorney, immediately," said Lisa calmly, a business card already in one hand. "Should I contact Yardley directly or the department to let them know one has been retained? She asked on her way inside to use the phone.

"The station, just call the main number and they'll sort it out." She smiled, tiredly. "Thank you so much, Lisa. We'll all chip in."

"We can worry about that later," Lisa assured her. They clasped hands briefly and Lisa briskly strode out.

Lisa taught college classes because she wanted to, not because she needed the money. Her family had bought up farmland during the depression and sold it decades later when the price per acre had multiplied exponentially. Then they invested all their cash with a local boy from Omaha, name of Warren Buffett, and nobody in her family ever needed to work a day job ever again.

Lorraine released us from her embrace with a whispered, "Please tell me there's fresh cold lemonade ready or I swear I will faint dead away!" She drew one hand dramatically across her brow.

"Not to worry, the lemonade fairies have been hard at work." The three of us slipped out the garage door and headed for the kitchen. We noticed Jules at the base of the driveway getting out the passenger door of a black Pontiac Trans Am.

It was driven by her boyfriend, Arthur. At least I figured it was, I'd never met him. They'd been an item for about six months. Jen and I figured that if it was serious, she'd eventually introduce him to Lorraine and the others. It hadn't happened yet.

Before Jules could make it up the drive, movement caught my eye and I turned to see Bast shooting out from the bushes like a rocket. She crossed the driveway and zoomed into the front yard. It was only because I was watching her that I noticed Dottie standing in the shadow of the overhang above the front porch.

Nobody ever used the front door but salespeople. We always came and went by the kitchen door. She saw me looking and started diligently digging around in her purse. She stepped out onto the still-hot driveway and waved a greeting to Jules.

"I must have left my reading glasses in my car," she said brightly. "I'll be right in."

Jules nodded and smiled, distractedly as she passed us. She didn't say anything, just continued to the garage, head down, brow furrowed. She fidgeted with the bracelet she wore on her left wrist. It was new, and she didn't seem entirely comfortable with it. She almost never wore jewelry of any kind, and this was a fancy tennis bracelet that didn't seem her style at all. Jules clearly had something pressing on her mind.

Lorraine and Jen were already in the kitchen, tending to the lemonade. I glanced back at Dottie. She'd walked to where her car was parked, under the elm tree out front. But she wasn't looking inside it for her glasses. She stood, in the grass on the passenger side of her car, intently looking further down the street.

Down the street and just around the corner to the left, the black Trans Am had pulled over in front of the Reynolds' house. The brake lights were lit up, so they weren't parked, just stopped. The driver's side window silently rolled down. Out of a nearby yard, a big black cat rocketed out into the street towards the Trans Am, Bast hot on its tail. The black cat dodged her and leaped neatly into the Trans Am's open window.

Bast stopped at the last second and jigged to her left, her eyes trained on the driver. The Trans Am rolled slowly down the street, the window closing, paying Bast no mind. I could have been wrong, but I thought I heard the sound of laughter.

I looked at Dottie who was staring at the scene, literally scratching her head. Then she opened the passenger door and sat. She closed the door, not all the way or she'd have cooked, but closed enough to conceal her actions from anyone walking by. From my vantage point higher up on the driveway, I could still see her dig down between the two front bucket seats and emerge with a brick phone.

Brick phones were precursors to mobile phones. Comparatively, they were enormous, awkward and heavy. It was literally like holding a brick to your head. *Why did Dottie have a brick phone?* I didn't know hardly anyone back then who had one, except my uncle who owned a car dealership and that Army friend of Mr. Rakow's who came to visit last spring. He'd stayed in after Vietnam and had become some big muckity-muck General or something.

But why would a retired Art History Professor need one? And why did she fib about leaving her glasses in the car, just so she could go watch Arthur drive away? And what in the world was the deal with Arthur and that black cat and Bast?

And was it my imagination or had I actually caught a glimpse of hot pink? Like the collar on the cat I'd seen sunning herself on the split-rail fence on my way home yesterday afternoon?

Curiouser and curiouser, as Alice would say. I ducked inside the kitchen door before Dottie could notice me staring. Jen handed me a tray and I went to the cupboard to load it up with glasses. The boys came up from the basement, Shadow and Tati on their heels.

David followed the dogs outside, but Jon stopped for a kiss, and got roped into holding the door as we schlepped out glasses and drinks. We filled them in as quickly as we could. I didn't have time to add the bit about Arthur and Dottie and the cat before Dottie reappeared, chatting with Mr. Rakow who had just arrived, freshly showered and shaved.

I bit my lip and opened my ears. Whatever was up, I didn't want to miss a thing.

Mr. Rakow held the door to the garage open for Dottie, and Tati and Shadow streaked in, nearly taking everyone out at the knees. Mr. Rakow made a clicking noise at Shadow who turned on a dime, rushed to sit at attention at Mr. Rakow's feet, and once released, jumped up to plant a slobbery kiss on his face before running back to play with Tati. David, Jon, Jen and I snaked past Mr. Rakow and he shut the door behind us against the still stifling heat.

The Coven had completed reloading the chandelier and it was hanging from its rope and pully system from the exposed rafters. Candles burned on all the tabletops as well, flickering slightly in the breeze of the window AC and the small fans now running in each corner. Groups of chairs had been pulled together here and there and the hum of conversation was louder than the racket of all the fans.

"How could *anyone* even think Miss Charlotte would be *able* to kill anyone?" Nicole agonized. "Especially a grown man as big as Viktor! She's no superhero ninja, for the love of the goddess, she's 5'6 and has a bad back!"

Rome and Deanne had spotted us the minute we came in with the drinks, and jumped up to help – and to get a glass. When the others saw where they were headed, a collective cheer went up and the conversation paused briefly while the witches took refreshment.

Elizabeth and Becky hung back, whispering and looking giddy. I wondered what mischief they had up their sleeves. Becky's black jeans were torn in so many places they were almost shorts, and her t-shirt was sleeveless, showing off arms made buff by hauling around heavy band equipment. Elizabeth never wore anything except black, form-fitting pants and flowing tops, finished off with combat boots. Her hair was purple today. It changed frequently. It was currently cut short, but she had a little braided tail over her left temple that hung down nearly to her waist.

Lisa came inside and Lorraine turned to her expectantly.

"There's an attorney on his way to the station now. He's to call here with news so I've brought the cordless out, if that's all right?" Lisa asked.

The general rule was no interruptions during Coven meetings, but this was obviously an exceptional circumstance. Lorraine nodded and beckoned her over.

"Did he say anything about how long they might keep her there, or if he thinks she'll be arrested?" Lorraine asked.

"That depends on whether or not they turn up any damning evidence in favor of their theory that Charlotte killed Viktor." Lisa said, solemnly. "They haven't found the murder weapon yet, so they asked for and received permission to search her house and car."

"Wait, she gave them permission so search her house and car?" Becky asked, aghast.

"She did!" Lisa said, her eyes twinkling. "According to the Coroner, the injury that killed Viktor was made with a scimitar. Specifically, an antique scimitar. So, assuming Miss Charlotte doesn't have a hot medieval Persian scimitar tucked up in her medicine closet, which she says she doesn't, they won't find anything and they won't have any cause to hold her. "

"A scimitar?" asked Dottie, half to herself. She sounded surprised.

"Of course there is no cause to hold her, because she's *innocent!* This is all just ridiculous!" declared Nicole hotly.

"How long will it take to search her house?" Elizabeth wondered.

"Oh goodness I hope they don't leave her a huge mess," groaned Deanne.

"Put the phone here," Lorraine directed Lisa. "Does it have a full charge? I'm sure the attorney will be calling soon." Jen took the phone from Lisa and put it in an empty glass from the drink tray to amplify the sound of the ringer, just to be safe.

"Guys!" Elizabeth said loudly into the conversational hubbub. "Guys, I've got a question. If Charlotte *didn't* kill Viktor to protect Shelly, then who killed him?" Voices were hushed. "And why?"

One second of silence fell into two then three and just as I heard someone draw a breath to speak, a loud knock rattled the door.

"Hello? Pizza delivery!" called a voice uncertainly from the other side.

A whoop went up from David and Jon, and Lorraine pulled cash from her pocket and stepped outside, handing boxes back in to David, Becky, and Pat who loaded up one table with the pizza boxes, paper plates and napkins.

Plates were filled and chairs pulled up to tables in short order. Pat, who'd been sitting in the back by herself picked up the conversation as soon as it was quiet enough for Elizabeth to hear her asking, "Do you have a theory?"

"I really don't," Elizabeth shook her head sounding both surprised and chagrined. "I met Shelly when I joined the Coven. She was the newest before me, so she sort of showed me the ropes. She never said anything to me about Viktor or any exes at all. But somebody killed Viktor, and if it wasn't Charlotte, then was it Shelly? And like, who even has scimitars?"

"Heh heh, well I could tell you a few stories, about *that!*" My eyes jumped from my notebook, which had come out the second Elizabeth started asking questions, to where Mr. Rakow was standing next to the lemonade jar, ladling more into his empty cup. His face was a little red and he looked very happy. I saw Becky wink at Elizabeth, who quirked a tiny smile.

"Scimitars, eh?" Pat mused over my shoulder. I jumped. Pat often made me jump. She was petite with brown hair and eyes. I'd never seen her wear any color besides black. She was quiet and rarely drew attention to herself. Especially when Lisa and Nicole were there together.

I felt sad for Pat's heartache over Nicole, but also, she made me nervous. Plus, I'd overheard Lorraine and Dottie talking one time, and I got the impression that Pat was an extremely powerful witch. She was also freaky smart. Her job at the University had something to do with genetics research.

There were times when the Coven felt like family to me, and there were other times when they felt like a band of escaped mega-supercharged convicts being wrangled by Lorraine and Dottie for the sake of world peace. I edged over to the end of the pizza table, where the guys had drawn up chairs. I tucked in next to Jon instead of getting myself another seat. Jon didn't seem to mind.

I put my chin on his shoulder and whispered, "I'd avoid the lemonade unless you want to catch a buzz," into his ear.

"So that's why Mr. Rakow went back for thirds!" Jon cracked a grin.

"I should tell Jen," I whispered, enjoying the smell of his warm skin.

"I'm sure she's got it well under control," Jon protested, tucking his non-pizza-eating arm securely around my waist. Sure enough, just then Jen and Jules carried in a big cooler I knew to be full of ice and canned sodas.

Through the briefly opened door, I spotted Bast, lounging in the shade of the garage roof overhang, her back to us, keeping watch.

Elizabeth, from her seat at the table nearest me, drank down the rest of her lemonade and wiped her mouth on the back of her hand. "So, when *did* Viktor enter the picture? Shelly joined the Coven almost exactly two years ago, right? And she was pretty new to town then, as I recall," she tossed the question out to everybody.

"He didn't find her until later last fall," Nicole took up her story where she'd left off in the kitchen. "He turned up at her mom's place unannounced one night, full of charming concern for her mother, who he'd never met." She rolled her eyes.

"What did she do?" asked Elizabeth, raising her brows at Nicole.

I wanted to know too, but I was briefly entranced by the absolutely flawless eyeliner wings she managed to paint. I was doing well to keep from sticking myself in the eye with the wand any time I tried it. I wondered if she'd give me makeup lessons.

"She called the cops!" Nicole said. "That's when Charlotte finally got the whole story from Shelly, and when the two of them got so close. Charlotte really helped her through a lot the last six months."

David perked up when she said that. I wondered what he was thinking.

"So did the police arrest him? After she called them?" Elizabeth pressed.

"He got a slap on the wrist for violating the restraining order. There was some loophole because the order was placed in another state," Nicole said, scowling.

"And then what?" Elizabeth asked.

"Well, it seems like he must have hung around, but if so, he kept a low profile, because Charlotte would have for sure told me if he'd showed up again. But, Shelly had her hands full with her mom last winter too, so there was plenty of other drama going on that Charlotte told me about," Nicole shook her head and widened her eyes.

Everyone had pulled their chairs in close. Paper plates of Valentino's Classic hamburger pizza were balanced on knees or nearby card tables and empty glasses of lemonade sat by every seat.

Oh boy.

"What other drama was going on?" Rome asked, her eyes alight.

"That's when they had all that trouble with the home health aide who was stealing from Shelly's mom!" Nicole recalled excitedly, draining her lemonade and catching the half-melted ice cubes in her mouth to crunch. I felt Jon shudder next to me. Aww, his poor sensitive ears.

"What got stolen?" Jules asked, a little sharply.

"At first, they thought some cash, maybe some pills, and then a strand of Shelly's great grandmother's pearls went missing. You were in on that, too weren't you, Dottie?" Nicole asked. "Didn't you have to go raise hell with their main office or whatever before they'd do anything about it?"

"I'm afraid I raised a little too much hell. In my zeal to see my dear old friend protected, I may have gotten her blacklisted. Shelly had a terrible time finding in-home help for Janet after that," Dottie sighed.

"I don't think it was that so much as Shelly just didn't really trust anybody but herself and Charlotte around her mom after that. Anyway, she went into hospice care in late December and passed just after the New Year."

Dottie raised her can of soda up in a toast. "To Janet. And to Shelly. Fine women who made their mark and will be keenly missed."

Glasses and cans were raised all around, and we drank in a moment of silence.

"I want to hear more about the thief," came Pat's voice, an unsettling rumble in the tone as if it suffered from disuse.

"She was kind of a wild girl, Charlotte said," replied Nicole, a note of gentleness meant for Pat in her tone. "With an odd name. Like Susie, but spelled strangely."

"Like, with an XZY at the end?" Ginny asked sharply.

"Yes!" Nicole cried.

"Oh, shit!" exclaimed Ginny.

And Jules.

And Becky.

And Pat.

"Okay, witches," Lorraine said, shaking her head. "Let's hear from each of you who knows this Siouxzy girl, starting with you, Ginny dearest." Her tone was as firm and decisive as it was loving. While she spoke, she leaned over, opened the cooler and without looking, pulled out an icy cold bottle of water and handed it to Ginny. Ginny took it gratefully. I was already getting the sense that "pregnant" and "summer heat" didn't go all that well together.

"She's a friend of Chuck's. She comes around sometimes, but she never hangs out. Chuck says she's too scared of the dogs," Ginny said dismissively, then frowned.

"I think she might have gone with him on his last trip down to Las Vegas." She took another pull of water while she considered that. "He usually takes Brutus with him, but he didn't that time. He seemed pissy about it, and Brutus was a great big baby all week without him."

I couldn't begin to imagine all the things Ginny was processing right then. I was pretty sure, though, that if Chuck had anything to do with either selling dogs for fighting or whatever this business was with Shelly, that he had some troubles coming his way via one angry, red-headed, pregnancy-hormone-fueled witch.

"What was that trip to Vegas about, do you know, Gin?" Lorraine asked gently.

"I bet I do," Jules said sadly.

"What is it, Jules?" Lorraine asked.

"They went out of town from May 15th to the 20th,

didn't they, Gin?" Jules asked.

Ginny nodded; eyebrows raised.

"Same time Arthur went down for one of his high-stakes poker games," Jules muttered.

"Yes. A big-time poker game. He was so geeked to be invited!"

"Chuck won big, didn't he?" Jules asked.

"He didn't say, exactly, but right after that he started getting lots of packages delivered, and not by the regular mail truck!" she blurted out, as if grateful to be able to say the words out loud.

"What kind of packages?" Dottie asked, sharply.

"All kinds, all different sizes of packages. Big, small, even round. But he never opened them in the house. It all went straight out to the horse barn where he has the dogs and his office and all," she said.

Oh, my. I'd sure love to have a look around in Chuck's horse barn!

"So, are you two thinking that Chuck and Arthur and this Siouxzy person went to Vegas together and did something shady?" Lorraine asked. "Something beyond just high stakes poker? Any ideas as to what they might have been up to?"

"If Siouxzy was in on it, it would have involved stealing something," Becky said decidedly.

"What's your story, Becky?" Lorraine asked. "What do you know about Siouxzy?"

"I know that if it isn't nailed down, it's fair game for her to light-finger. And if it *is* nailed down, she's just gonna take that as a challenge," Becky said flatly.

"Do you know her well?" Lorraine asked.

"I was on the street with her for a few months, before I met Dottie," she said looking down. That time she'd been adrift had impacted Becky powerfully. I got the sense from her, sometimes, that she wasn't sure real sure how to act now, as a member of this Coven. Sometimes she seemed defensive, like she was going to face reprisal or judgement, but I'd never ever seen any of the witches give her anything but kindness and understanding.

Lorraine had an arm around her shoulder before she'd even finished the sentence. Becky grinned, for a second unguarded. I was reminded that she was only a couple of years older than us.

"So, she's a desperate woman, and a skilled thief," said Lorraine.

"And she knows magic," said Becky. "I'm pretty sure of it, anyway. She never talked about it, though."

"It's worse," came that low gravelly voice from the shadows. Pat looked up from the napkin she'd been shredding in her lap and looked around at us.

"Worse, how?" Dottie stared at Pat, her normally joyful expression replaced by one I'd never seen. She wasn't mad, but super serious, and super in-charge. I wondered again about that phone in her car.

"She knows plenty of magic, that one. She's been practicing all her life. Siouxzy is a witch," Pat said flatly. "Born and bred. And that bloodline is one you all know. Siouxzy's a *Katze*."

Lorraine cocked her head dubiously. "*Katze*? You're kidding, right? Isn't that just an old babushkas tale?" Lorraine asked.

"No, she is quite correct," Dottie said calmly. "They existed, and if Pat's information is correct," here she eyed Pat who nodded, solemnly. "They are still among us."

David literally raised his hand at this point. He and Mr. Rakow had settled down on the rug with Tati and Shadow. Mr. Rakow was sitting comfortably up against a shelf nearly stacked with plastic tubs full of garage sale supplies. Shadow sat next to him and licked his nose occasionally when Mr. Rakow's slow blinks lengthened into the post-spiked-lemonade-nap zone.

David sat cross-legged with Tati curled up in his lap looking for all the world like a little kid at storytime. "What's a *Katze*?" David asked. Mr. Rakow snickered unexpectedly and Shadow's tail thumped the ground. Lorraine crossed to the shelves, opened a tub, extracted a big floor pillow and tossed it to Mr. Rakow. I swear he caught it with his eyes closed.

"*Katze* are, according to lore," Lisa supplied, looking up from her knitting, "a cast-off branch of a Romani family from Germany. The story goes that back sometime in the 8th century, they were banished for practicing black magic. Specifically, ailuranthropy."

"I lur what?" David asked.

"They used magic to turn themselves into cats," I supplied, looking directly at Dottie.

"Impossible!" Jules exclaimed. "Cannot be done!"

"It *can* be done," Pat said decisively.

"How do you know?" Jules asked, eyeing her closely.

"Because Katze are my kin on my mother's side, and I've heard stories about Siouxzy since she was brought to the States, orphaned at age three, her entire family dead in a tragic fire," Pat said, darkly.

"Oh, the poor child!" Deanne cried.

"It was foolishness to bring her here!" Pat hissed through clenched teeth.

"Why do you say that?" Deanne asked, surprised.

"Because Siouxzy started that fire."

Excited murmurs bubbled around the room. Deanne got up and moved over to the empty seat by Pat. They didn't talk, just sat together.

Jen strolled over to the pizza table from her spot near Lorraine, and leaned over to whisper in my ear. "That vision, the one from the amber? It's starting to make sense now."

"What? What are you thinking?" I whispered back.

"I think I was seeing the attack through Siouxzy's eyes, when she was in cat form. I've had ghosts speak through me, I've seen space from the eye of a meteorite, but I've never experienced anything as vicious and," she shook her head, searching for the right word. "I've never felt anything that *wild*."

"Wild like crazy?" Jon asked, "or wild like uncivilized?"

"Both," Jen stated unequivocally. "Absolutely both."

"Don't say anything yet, not until you talk to mom," Jon cautioned.

"Right. Thus, the whispering," Jen whispered. She took some pizza, grabbed a can of soda out of the cooler, and returned to her seat by her mom.

If Jen was interpreting her vision correctly, and Siouxzy killed Shelly, well, I didn't know exactly how the Coven would react. I was happy to leave that powder keg to Lorraine.

"Wait," drawled Mr. Rakow, eyes closed, from his position on the floor pillow next to Shadow. I jumped. I thought he'd dozed off. "Is Siouxzy a super powerful witch? Or is she an insane pyromaniac?"

"Both. It's the magic," Pat said. "It's dark magic. The kind that can only be powered by blood sacrifice. And because she's a hereditary witch, from a line of witches going back at least thirteen hundred years, that lineage of dark magic has taken a hereditary toll. The children born into those families almost always struggle with serious mental illnesses." Deanne put a hand on Pat's arm. Pat sighed. "Depression and mania are common. Pyromania, extreme paranoia and even schizophrenia are all liberally sprinkled throughout the bloodlines."

"So, okay. We're thinking that Chuck and Arthur and Siouxzy are all in some kind of criminal gang together, and that Siouxzy is not only a thief, but a powerful witch, an ailuranthrope, and also mega-unbalanced. But then where does Viktor fit in? Or does he?" Elizabeth asked, tucking her long braid of hair behind one ear and sipping her newly full glass of lemonade meditatively.

Lorraine looked meaningfully at Dottie, who sighed.

"Sisters, I have a confession to make," said Dottie gently.

I flipped to a new page in my notebook and I am pretty sure I licked the tip of my pen in anticipation. I swear I don't do that kind of silly-ass Jimmy Olsen stuff anymore, hardly ever.

All eyes were on Dottie. She settled herself in her chair and faced us all.

"After I retired from Wesleyan, I was approached by a Federal Agency that concerns itself with International Art theft. They wanted my expertise on a case they were working, an obscure Portuguese artist I'd published a study of some years before," she trailed off. "One thing led to another and I've been working with them on and off, consulting since."

"Ohmigod!" Elizabeth erupted. "You're a secret agent! You're like, Indiana Jones!"

Dottie laughed. "Not quite, but I sure do like his hat! Look, the short story here is that my team has been looking at a group that's been popping up here and there on the scene, making a name for themselves with some extremely valuable pieces. When I realized that Chuck and Arthur might be involved, I made my full disclosure to them, letting them know that my objectivity was compromised in this situation. She nodded to Jules and Ginny respectfully, and shared a knowing look with Rome.

"My boss took me off the case, but I continued to keep an eye on Siouxzy. That's how I know Viktor was in on it from the beginning. He came to Nebraska to find Shelly, but Siouxzy sniffed him out immediately as a fellow grifter, and she's the one that introduced Viktor to Chuck and Arthur.

"Ginny," Dottie said, glancing at her watch. "I'll tell you this now, because it's a done deal. There was a raid on Chuck's place today. Those packages he's been receiving are stolen art from jobs around the world. Chuck and Arthur are part of a syndicate of smugglers. They've been playing hot potato with stolen goods, transferring items between collectors all over the globe.

"It's not the only scam they're running, but it is the place where they all intersect," Dottie said sadly. "I'm sorry, Ginny, Jules. I was planning to tell you all last week, after I'd quit the investigation, but then Shelly disappeared and I was advised to keep my mouth shut until we knew more. I'm very sorry this has landed so close to home.

"And Pat," Dottie stood and walked slowly over to her. "We do not judge anyone on the actions of their family. You are a member of this Coven in good standing. If your family passed magic on to you that is dangerous or misunderstood, we are here to help you understand and work with what you know. Your magic is a reflection of your soul, and all of us here know that your soul is healing from your past, and is becoming stronger and better for it."

"Sister." The word was spoken quietly by all the witches in the room, and the air vibrated.

Pat looked up at Dottie, then around and everyone. She nodded and smiled a small, relieved smile.

"I have more questions," Elizabeth spoke into the silence that followed.

"And those are?" Rome asked.

"What was at Shelly's house that was valuable enough to tempt art thieves," Elizabeth held up one finger, then a second, "and where is it now?"

"I think I may be able to help answer that question." The door had opened silently, and in the doorway stood Diane, thirteenth member of the Coven, who had been down on her farm in Kansas since Friday morning.

Diane was dressed in faded khaki pants, a long-sleeved white linen shirt and an army green vest. Between her pants and vest, she was sporting several dozen pockets. Her thick black hair was cut in a shag once every six months whether it needed it or not.

"Shelly came out to my place Wednesday morning with a plant she said she'd found at Wilderness Park, walking with Tati. She thought, and she was correct, that it was a western prairie fringed orchid." She turned to Ginny and said, "platanthera praeclara."

Ginny's eyebrows shot up appreciatively.

"Very rare," Ginny informed the rest of us. "May be on the endangered list soon. Why did she move it?" Ginny asked Diane.

"It was over by the bridge they're repairing this summer, off So. 14th St. She dug it out of the shadow of a tractor's wheel," Diane replied.

"Whew!" Ginny exclaimed, clearly relieved the orchid had been rescued. "So, she wanted to plant it at your place?"

"Yes. She knew I was working with some other wetlands flowers, so the thought maybe it would be okay with me."

"So, you planted it in your yard?" Ginny asked.

"Well, she did it. She insisted, said she was already covered in mud. And right after I showed her where to put it, Tati suddenly and mysteriously learned how to open my gate and let Bailey and the boys out!"

I turned to Jon and said, in my best British detective voice, "Ah yes, the classic dog distraction." He grinned and held me closer.

"By the time I got everyone inside and the gate shut, Shelly was done planting. I'll admit, I thought it was, what do you kids call it? *Hinky?*"

Four thumbs went up.

"I thought it was hinky then, now I think she must have buried more than just the roots of that plant. And if whatever is buried in my garden is going to bring all the crooks to my yard, I have to say, she must have been pretty desperate."

"Is it still there?" Jules demanded.

"Presumably, yes. I didn't have time to do anything with it just then, and there was so much happening with the Coven meeting and the storm damage out at the farm, truth be told I didn't even think about it again until last night. I came straight here from the road; I haven't even been home yet."

"Maybe we'd better get over there and figure out just exactly what Miss Shelly planted!" Elizabeth exclaimed, setting down her empty lemonade glass and getting to her feet, with only a little wobbliness.

Just then, the cordless phone rang, its sound weirdly amplified by the glass it sat inside. Lorraine snatched it out.

"Hello? Yes, she is, just a sec," she handed the phone off to Lisa.

"This is Lisa, yes, Jack, yes? Okay great! Now grab a pen. I'm going to give you the address we'll all be at in 20 minutes. I want you to meet us there, and bring Charlotte! I'll explain when we get there."

Lorraine grabbed the phone back before Lisa could say goodbye.

"Jack, please relay that information to Officer Yardley or Officer Rogers as well, thank you!"

Jen drove me and the boys, including an only slightly groggy Mr. Rakow and the dogs, in Clint. Ginny and Lorraine, the only two who had passed on the spiked lemonade, drove the others. Diane led the way.

I flipped back and forth through my notes trying to coordinate my thoughts. "We now know that somehow or another Shelly or her mom had something of interest to this gang of art thieves. We think whatever it was probably got spotted by Siouxzy when she was working there, and that she cultivated Viktor as a partner at least partially in hopes of getting her hands on it after she was fired. We know they recently made a trip to Vegas and the contraband was getting stored in Chuck's horse barn, which has since been raided. But what we still don't know is a lot!" I groaned.

"Spell it out, Ang," Jen said from the driver's seat.

"What happened that night when Shelly came home? Was Viktor there? Or was he already dead? And who killed him? And if Shelly was escaping in her car, who or what was she running from? Was it just Siouxzy? Or was it the others as well? We think it was Siouxzy the cat in the car with her, but was she the only one?

"What exactly went down? Say Shelly came home, upset from the argument with Charlotte, and started to go into the house. Siouxzy was there, and Viktor too. Maybe all of them! Maybe they confronted her. Maybe she tried to get away and Siouxzy jumped in her car? I have so many questions!" I groaned.

"Will finding this, this valuable whatever it is that Chuck and Arthur and Siouxzy are so hot to get their hands on, will that get us any closer to finding out how Shelly and Viktor died?" Jon asked.

"I'm afraid it might," I said thoughtfully.

"Why are you afraid?" Jon asked.

"Because," I said slowly. "The three of them are out there right now, and we're on our way to go dig up what they want so badly that two people have already died for it."

Crap.

It was just starting to get dark when we arrived at Diane's. Her place was on three acres, just east of town. She was one of the last few homeowners in the area who hadn't sold out to developers who would eventually turn all of this farmland into suburbs.

The house was nice, an old two-story white farmhouse with a huge wrap-around porch. But being a Master Gardner, the real treasure was Diane's gardens. Our convoy of cars turned into the long, straight gravel driveway along which Diane had planted cottonwoods interspersed with ones she called hornbeams.

The front yard was graced with smaller, more ornamental dogwoods and crab apples. We pulled up to the gate that led to her fenced flower gardens. It was fenced both so her dogs could run without crossing the road and also to keep deer out. For the latter, the fence had to be seven feet high, but Diane had enough unique and endangered plants, she was willing to go to the trouble for his space.

It was a space about half the size of a football field, and a creek ran through it, away from the house, past the greenhouse and down the slope through the trees. It was a wonderland. She'd created intertwined spaces for full sun and shade plants, and most recently she'd been creating the wetlands in a dappled shady spot near the bridge her woodworker boyfriend had built. A gravel path, wide enough for two people to walk comfortably abreast meandered among wildflowers and native grasses. Ash trees and mulberries shaded the path as it approached the bridge.

Diane let us to the spot in a protected glade near the bridge where she'd instructed Shelly to plant the orchid. It appeared undisturbed. It didn't look like I thought an orchid would. Instead of one single bloom on a long stalk, there were half a dozen or so blossoms on one stalk. Its petals were white and feathery and the whole thing sort of reminded me of stick drawings of a person with a yellowish face.

We all crowded around while Diane delicately scooped at the soil around the delicate flower with her bare hands, careful not to disturb the roots. Only a few inches down, her fingers struck something foreign. Carefully, like an archaeologist, she drew out a package wrapped in a black cloth. She carefully unwound the cloth to reveal a small, carved wooden box.

It was only about the size of a cassette tape, and made of a shiny polished wood that glowed deeply black in the fading light. Radiating out from the center of the box in Diane's palm were thin strips of golden inlay in an artful sunburst pattern.

Lorraine reached for it and Dottie snatched her hand back

"Don't open it, not out here. The moon is too close to full!"

"Dottie, what do you know about this thing?"

Lorraine pressed her.

"I know it's powerful, and it could be dangerous. We need to consult with Maka before we unintentionally do anything that cannot be undone."

Diane wrapped the cloth back around the little box and held it out to Lorraine and Dottie. That's when a big black cat with a pink collar dropped down on her from the tree above her head and attacked.

It was the same cat I'd seen on the fence rail and jumping into Arthur's car. It had to be Siouxzy! Had she been following *me* on Friday? Why? For sure, Bast had been onto her from the start!

Before anyone had time to intervene, Siouxzy clawed and bit at Diane's arm, hand, and face trying to get her to let go of the box. Diane's long sleeves were little protection, and when Siouxzy went berserk on her face, Diane threw up her hands and rolled.

The dogs were all going bananas too. Shadow, Tati, and Diane's three; Jim, Bailey and Huck, which was great, but super confusing. The dogs were barking and yipping at the tops of their lungs, Siouxzy was howling and screeching when she didn't have a mouthful of Diane. Diane's dogs were only interested in protecting her, and they were getting in the way of the shouting, stumbling Coven members who wanted to help.

When Diane rolled, a shimmer of magic vibrated the air around us, and suddenly Diane was pinned. Not by an over-large housecat, but by a 150 lb. woman, barefoot, wearing a black t-shirt tucked into black jeans.

Siouxzy looked younger than her 23 years, with raven black hair and a round, almost cherubic face. There was nothing cherubic about her expression though. The glint in her eye and the snarl on her face made her look both ferocious and strangely gleeful.

"Give it to me, bitch!" she screamed and then laughed. A high-pitched keening laugh that made my skin crawl and my 'flight' instinct insist that *anywhere but here* was lovely this time of year.

She wrenched the box out of Diane's hand. I heard a *crack* and Diane screamed. Siouxzy dropped the box down the front of her t-shirt, and gave Shadow, who had managed to get through the fray a sharp elbow to the head that set him back a step. Then she twisted and leapt straight up, and with another shimmer of magic, she dug her claws into the overhead branch and in a flash disappeared up into the branches.

Deanne, Nicole and Lisa surrounded Diane and began assessing her wounds. I heard Lisa say, "broken" and "hospital".

David and Mr. Rakow had separated Shadow and Tati from Diane's three and they and Jen were circling outward, looking up into the trees, trying to get a bead on Siouxzy. I was about to join them when Jon tugged on my belt loop.

"Angie, behind us. Someone's coming," he hissed.

I spun, but I was already too late. Two men sauntered down the path towards us. One brandished a shotgun in one hand and a handgun in the other, like some kind of red neck gangster. The other guy looked seriously dangerous. He was dressed in utilitarian black pants, boots and a t-shirt. He held his handgun with ease, but also with respect.

"Everybody can just relax. Nobody's going anywhere," Chuck called out, waving his shotgun back and forth, indicating our entire group. Those of us he could see anyway, in the fading light. Jen, David and Mr. Rakow had melted away into the trees the minute Jon had identified the threat and focused my eyes, and his sight on them. Jon and I stood very still where we were, just barely out of their line of sight, camouflaged amongst the branches of a Douglas fir.

The Coven had coalesced around Diane and her dogs. They stood in a circle, all with their eyes on Diane and their backs to Chuck and Arthur, with two exceptions. Ginny and Jules faced the two men head on.

Jules looked brokenhearted and stiff, her shaggy hair limp, her usual bright energy felt grey like iron. Ginny just looked pissed.

"Ginny, honey," Chuck drawled. "I don't know what you think you're doing here, but you need to get your cute little ass out of this mess and go on home. I'll deal with you later." He motioned with his handgun, indicating that she should go back up the path towards the cars.

"Chuck honey," Ginny drawled right back at him, "You need to kiss the hell off! This business you're tied up in is way worse than even you know. You think this," she motioned at his gun, "toting that thing around and stealing shit – you think this makes you a tough guy? You couldn't be more wrong! And let me tell you something else!" Sparks flew all around her. Chuck swallowed nervously. "If I find a single hair out of place on any one of those pups you sold last week when I go to take them back, I will end you myself!"

Chuck spluttered and looked like he was about to argue but was having trouble gathering his thoughts. I'd have recommended against that last beer he had on the way over here, had he asked. He didn't. His sputtering retorts were cut short when Siouxzy slinked down a tree behind the men and sashayed over to them, her tail swinging. She approached Chuck first, who instantly shut up and looked terrified.

Satisfied, she sauntered over to Arthur and rubbed

his leg. I'm pretty sure I could hear Jules' teeth grinding from where I stood. Another shimmer of magic and Siouxzy's human form unfurled against Arthur's side. He looked at her sternly and held out his hand. She pulled out the neckline of her t-shirt and winked at him invitingly.

Barf

Without hesitating, Arthur reached in and snatched the box out of Siouxzy's shirt. He shook it out of its cloth wrapping and nodded. He dropped it into his shirt pocket, and deftly secured the button closed. She giggled and snuggled up against him. He stood stiffly, but didn't push her away. He looked at Jules and shrugged. His dark eyes betrayed absolutely no emotion.

Jules pulled the sparkly tennis bracelet off that she'd been wearing uncomfortably for the last couple of weeks. Jen and I had spotted it right away, but she'd never offered any explanation for it, and I had more than once caught her picking at it like it itched.

She pulled it off her left wrist with her right hand and held it up. He frowned, confused. Jules whispered something I couldn't hear, and the bracelet changed from shiny gold and sparkly diamonds, to something black and gooey, like tar. She turned her hand over and the goop dripped down off her fingers onto the gravel pathway, steaming slightly and stinking of sulfur.

That's when the rest of the witches, who *of course* had been spellcasting quietly this entire time while Ginny and Jules stalled, all threw their hands up in the air in unison, and *WOOSH!*

Both men were suddenly whisked upwards about six feet in the air, given a quick spin on their vertical axes and left hanging midair, upside down. Siouxzy's reflexes were apparently as catlike as the rest of her, because she sensed the spell coming at them and fled before it touched her. She leaped away, changing once again back to her cat form.

The men both yelped in surprise. Chuck immediately dropped both his weapons into the dirt and continued to spin slowly, upside down, yelling and swearing, desperately trying to grab his weapons, but unable to reach.

Arthur, no less freaked out, kept his cool, and his weapon. But not for long. Jules approached Arthur slowly and deliberately, her eyes never leaving his center mass. He aimed as well as he could from his precarious position and fired. His first shot went wild, then his second and third. Each time he fired, the recoil sent his body spinning and jerking out of control. Every muscle tensed, he strained to line up for another try, and then yelped and dropped his gun like it was on fire.

"You lied to me," Jules said in a low, calm voice that belied the fury she must have been feeling. "You lied, and you stole, and by the goddess if you harmed Shelly in any way, that harm will return to you threefold. I will personally see to it."

Arthur gasped, not at her words, I don't think, but at his weapon which lay where he'd dropped it, in the grass near Chuck's two. The three of them were smoking and starting to look kind of – melty. Rome appeared at Jules' shoulder, and with the flick of one hand, all three guns zipped across the grass, leaving scorch marks as they went, and splashed down in the creek. I could hear the hiss of steam from where Jon and I stood.

Lorraine stood suddenly and clapped twice. Both men went stiff as boards. Chuck's swearing was silenced. They swayed slightly continuing to hover six feet above the ground. Lorraine approached Arthur and delicately unbuttoned his shirt pocket. The box slipped down before Lorraine could catch it and fell open.

"No! Don't let it!" exclaimed Dottie, frantically.

Lorraine snatched the box out of the grass, and passed her hand all around, searching. "It's empty! There's nothing inside!" She exclaimed.

"What?" Dottie cried.

"Oh no!" Diane exclaimed.

A sound from overhead made us all jump. Siouxzy, perched on the branch of an ash tree twenty feet overhead had seen everything and she was not a happy kitty. The sound she made was way more wildcat than domesticated. I've heard bobcats screaming in the woods before, and that's a sound that'll curl your toes for sure. This was worse.

The hairs on the back of my neck didn't just stand up, they threatened to revolt.

Then she took off.

"Don't let her go!" Pat's agonized scream jolted me into motion.

"Angie! That way!" Jon pointed, unseeing towards the fence line where the creek exited the property.

I ran.

I was grateful to have opted for tennies over flip flops, but the sharp prairie grasses sliced across my bare legs as I ran. Long pants and bug spray would have been awfully nice. I felt Jon *hitchhiking* along, turning my eyes, directing me across the darkening field towards Jen and David. I'd be lucky not to break an ankle.

I heard Shadow's sharp insistent barking. They'd treed her. The tree she was in was the closest of any to the fence, and it was surely too far for her to jump from. From that distance, any normal cat could never make the fence. Not even on a good day. Of course, she was no normal cat.

I thought she might try to retrace her steps, but something in the next tree closest to her was growling and spitting. *Pat?* I wondered.

Both Shadow and Tati pawed and growled and yipped, leaping around the base of the tree. Mr. Rakow had picked up a long branch and was stabbing it upwards. Siouxzy hissed and spat. David and Jen saw me coming and raised their arms. I felt the stone necklace under my t-shirt warm.

I skidded into place, nearly losing my balance on the uneven earth. I flung both arms wide, catching my balance along with the red beam of light from David's necklace in my left and the green one from Jen in my right.

"Up! High!" Jen sang out, just as Siouxzy made her attempt for the fence.

I focused my thoughts upward, joining theirs, spreading the focus of our combined power from a line into a plane, stretching up, up, up as high as we could push it.

Siouxzy jumped. It was an Olympics worthy attempt. She rushed to the end of the branch nearest the fence, gaining as much speed as possible.

If she made it, she was home free. I knew in my heart, if our barrier wasn't high enough, or strong enough, she might make it. I watched her powerful legs gather for the leap.

She was *going* to make it!

I PUSHED my magic upwards and bolstered it with thoughts of Shelly. Her musical laugh, he encyclopedic knowledge of artists from all over the world, her seemingly endless collection of goofy sunhats, heavy on the pastels and ribbons, and her sweet, kind heart. I imagined her scattering those tiny polished pieces of amber – blessed by the Coven – blanketing anyone who came to her home with blessings and goodwill. She was so kind, and so wonderful. And she was taken away from us by thieves.

Arcs of deep blue power shot through the magic emanating from me, through my stone necklace, and was met by Jen's powerful wall of green and David's fiery red.

And SMACK.

She hit our wall with all the force she'd put into that jump, headfirst.

Down, she slid. Stunned, down into the grass.

The dogs bolted after her.

"Shadow, hold!" Mr. Rakow yelled. "Hold!"

Hold was Shadow's command to grasp prey in his jaws gently and bring it, relatively unharmed, to Mr. Rakow. German Shepherds are not typically trained in the ways of hunting dogs, but Shadow knew more than most dogs.

Tati, however, did not.

Tati got to the cat first, and grabbed her by the neck and shook. Hard.

"Tati No!" I yelled, running as fast as I could. "Tati!" That shimmer of magic appeared again, but weaker. Tati jumped back as the figure of the cat changed once again. When Siouxzy's human form appeared, there was a trickle of blood running down her cheek. She struggled to stand, and still, I could hear her chanting in Latin. Whatever she had lined up, I bet it wouldn't be good.

Tati and Shadow faced her, staying just out of reach, snarling and snapping their teeth. She lifted one arm and drew in her breath to shout. Mr. Rakow darted up behind her with his big branch and smacked the back of her head like it was a baseball and he was swinging for the fences.

Siouxzy was out.

Epilogue

The attorney Lisa had called for Charlotte didn't just tell Officer Yardley where we were, I'm pretty sure he told half the town. Or at least half the town seemed to be parked in Diane's driveway at any rate. Blocking in Clint and the rest of the cars we'd driven over in were Chuck's pickup, Arthur's Trans Am, and a beat up old blue VW Beetle with 3-county plates. Behind those were about six police cruisers, a fire truck, and an ambulance.

The Coven had tied up Chuck and Arthur and let them drop before the first officers arrived. They were removed to two of the various squad cars in the driveway. Siouxzy got the ambulance, but not before Dottie, Lorraine, and Pat draped her in a set of spells that should, they hoped, inhibit her magic for a day or two. They needed to buy some time to figure out what they were going to do about the problem that was Siouxzy.

EMT's checked out Diane's hand and told her in no uncertain terms that she had broken fingers. Lisa and Nicole took her to the ER in Diane's pickup, the only vehicle currently not blocked in by emergency responders.

Between the police investigation, the Federal art smuggling probe, the ASPCA's investigation into the dog fighting ring, and of course the insurance, it took most of a year before everything was sorted out. But Chuck got them well on the way to figuring out what was going in that first night.

Ginny's new ex spilled his guts almost immediately to the police in return for the promise of a lighter sentence. He detailed all he knew about Arthur's organization that included small time thieves like himself in over a dozen states, some lifting valuables, others stashing them around in small towns or out on vacant farmland and waiting for the right amount of time had passed before they could them on the black market. Arthur managed the inventory and the sales, his crews of thieves and drivers worked for a cut and of course anything that happened to *fall off the truck* in the commission of their thefts. Arthur always wanted specific items, and he actually encouraged his flunkies to steal indiscriminately in some cases to muddy the water.

Siouxzy was one of his best thieves. It was due to the quantity of items she'd stolen that Arthur decided to hire Chuck to store the extra inventory until it could be moved out to another location. Between what she'd procured in the last month or so, plus the haul they'd acquired on their high-stakes poker trip to Las Vegas, Chuck's horse barn was full to bursting with cash and illicit goods when the police raided it earlier that day.

Lisa's attorney called several weeks later to give her an update on the case, and she insisted he come to her at Lorraine's so the entire Coven could hear the report at once.

Jen and I settled into seats around the garage. It was still summer, still hot, but since midsummer, the heat seemed to have lost its teeth. It squawked and hollered and made the days hot and the nights genuinely unpleasant but we all knew that September was a just breath away. The giant garage AC labored gamely on and we tucked our sweating iced tea glasses under our chairs so they wouldn't get knocked over as the witches bustled around.

The boys were outside with Tati and Shadow. They'd wait until the last minute to come in and hear the lawyer, and they'd be the first to scoot out again once they'd heard the story.

Lisa came in with the attorney and spent a minute or two introducing him around and getting him seated near a table where he could open his briefcase and spread out his notes. I observed his stylishly conservative outfit and practical briefcase, and guessed him to be young, but not rookie young. He was kind of cute, in a, some-cute-toddler's-dad-at-the-park kind of way.

"Whenever you're ready, Jack," Lisa said. "Everyone is here."

Certainly, nearly everyone was. Nicole sat with Dottie, who had given up her rocker to Ginny, and Lorraine. They were keeping a seat free for Lisa. Nicole's only concession to the heat was that under her many layers of gauzy black skirts and capes, her feet were bare of everything but jewelry. Lorraine leaned gracefully towards Dottie, who tilted her head, smiling, her blue eyes alight with good humor as they spoke quietly, under the general noise.

Nicole had asked if Charlotte shouldn't be allowed to be there as well. Lisa reminded her that there were some legal ramifications at play and they'd keep Miss Charlotte updated as they were able.

Deanne, Pat, Becky and Elizabeth occupied seats at another folding table. Deanne sported one of Wham's oversized, white "Choose Life" t-shirts and jeans. Hers was the sole non-black ensemble worn at that table. Elizabeth and Pat seemed relaxed to the point of boredom, while Becky was nervously picking at her sleeves.

Rome, Jules, Diane, and Ginny occupied chairs at the back. Rome and Ginny sported bright sundresses and Diane was rocking her signature khaki and linen vibe. Jules had on faded jeans with holes and shredded hems. On her feet were worn leather huarache sandals. They were unlike any you could get at the mall here, because she'd gotten them from a tiny town in Mexico. She'd only just returned from spending a couple of weeks hiking in Los Tuxtlas Biosphere Reserve with a friend who was also a healer. She'd taken off the morning after the Coven's ceremony for Shelly, which was, I guess, pretty intense. She looked tired, but happy.

That had been an intense night for the four of us, too. The Coven's ceremony was private, witch business. We were happy to give them space, and happy that Lorraine and Dottie seemed to have everything under control. I was quite sure there was more going on than Lorraine or Dottie was letting on, and that was fine by me. Coven business was Coven business. Just like our business was sometimes just ours.

We'd driven out to one of our favorite haunts. There was an old, one-room schoolhouse north of town where you could park just out of sight of the road. We took some blankets, a little bottle of schnapps, and some bug spray and the four of us lay on our backs, our feet marking the cardinal directions, our heads just inches apart.

We made a toast to Shelly and passed around the hooch. It wasn't enough to get the four of us more than mildly silly, but it did seem to loosen our tongues some.

"Do you think they caught her?" I asked, relishing the warmth of the schnapps in my belly. "The night Siouxzy escaped from the County lockup. Do you think the Coven caught her?"

"I think they did," David said, much satisfaction in his tone. "I think they took care of business."

"Or they're doing so tonight," Jen suggested.

I sighed. This whole thing had me moody and

introspective. What's more, I think the only reason the others hadn't called me on my mood was that they were feeling it too.

"What do we do when it happens to us?" I said, carefully trying out the words, afraid of what might happen when they were spoken aloud, but knowing they needed to be said.

"When one of us," Jen began.

"Dies," David said bluntly. "What do we do when one of us dies?"

"You three do very dangerous work," Jon said quietly. He reached for my hand and found it, reaching for his.

"We do. It's logical to think it could happen to us," Jen said simply.

"And then what? What happens then?" I asked.

"Revenge," David said firmly.

"A measured response," Jen said. "An equal and opposite response."

"Screw that," David countered. "If something happens to any of you, I will burn it down. I will burn it all to the ground to avenge you. You can count on it."

"I can't imagine Lorraine or the Guardian being totally on board with that plan," I said.

"Screw that too, Ang," David said harshly. "I won't," his breath hitched. "I can't lose you." He drew in a long, shuddery breath. "Any of you," he whispered.

I sat up and turned around, sitting cross legged and facing the center of the circle. My friends did the same. "Let's make sure we're not giving anybody the opportunity," I said decidedly. "If we all live, then nobody has to avenge our deaths."

"I don't hate that plan," Jon seconded.

"To not dying!" Jen declared and sent the schnapps

around one last time.

"Cheers," said David, somberly.

We drank. And then we fell silent again and watched the stars.

Really, the only piece of Coven business outstanding after that night's ceremonies, was the missing artifact. Hopefully, Jack the attorney had some good news on that front.

Jack sat on his folding chair in Lorraine's garage and opened his leather briefcase and took out a binder which he proceeded to glance at from time to time as he talked.

"Some of Chuck's statement to the police has become available to me as it relates to Shelly's death," Jack began, and everyone quieted. "I also have information from interviews our office has conducted with interested parties as part of our inquiry into Miss Shelly's death, and to find and recover any and all objects that may have been stolen from her home, at your behest." He looked around and nodded at the assembled. Lisa had set it up so that the entire Coven was listed as Jack's firm's "client" in this case so that everyone was privy to all the information and all of this was confidential.

"Our interviews with Charlotte indicate that Miss Shelly never divulged to her any sort of particularly valuable items of jewelry her mother may have had, but that she had once mentioned an item that likely had some value to occult or rarity collectors," he said, relying strictly on the non-hinky description of what was possibly a powerful magical artifact.

"Inquiries to the families that Siouxzy had worked for over the past year as an in-home health aide revealed a trail of thefts from the homes of vulnerable people," Jack went on. "Thefts that were not discovered right away by family members who only visited, but didn't live in.

"According to Chuck's statement, Siouxzy was angry because she was sure there was an item of some value in the home, and once Shelly came home to live with her mother, Siouxzy was prevented from finding it. He said Siouxzy obsessed over the situation, and accused Shelly of practicing witchcraft in order to keep her from finding the item."

"Which, of course, she was," I whispered to Jen.

Jen nodded. "The amber."

"She sensed the danger from Siouxzy," I said in her ear. "The amber was one way of diffusing ill intent. I'm sure it wasn't the only thing she was doing, but it would have been enough to throw her off her game." Lorraine gave us a look and we hushed.

"Chuck said that Siouxzy threatened to kill Shelly more than once in his presence," Jack said.

Pat hung her head. Deanne put a hand on her shoulder.

"Chuck also stated that while Siouxzy had been the one to bring Viktor in on their activities, she seemed to lose patience with him over the situation with Shelly. She'd been barred from the house by this point, of course. She wanted him to come with her when she broke into the house to see if he could find what she claimed was being magically concealed from her. Viktor was hesitant, Chuck said. He put her off several times, until Siouxzy threatened him.

"Siouxzy told Chuck on that Wednesday night, the 10th of June, that she knew from surveilling Shelly's activities, she would be gone until late. She and Viktor went to the house but again, found nothing. Siouxzy told Chuck afterwards she believed that Viktor had gotten there first and was holding out on her. They argued in the garage.

"The scimitar used to kill Viktor was found in

Siouxzy's stolen VW Beetle. Chuck indicated that it was from a cache of knockoff antiques that she'd lifted before she'd had Arthur around to tell her what was valuable and what was a cheap copy. She didn't care that it was a fake," Chuck said, "She liked it because she said it was like a cat's claw. He said she had a real thing for cats."

Pat rubbed her temples and sighed, shaking her head.

"Siouxzy told Chuck that she'd just hidden Viktor's body when Shelly got home. She said that she and Shelly argued and she threatened her with the scimitar as well, but Shelly managed to get back into her car with Tati and back out of the garage."

Here Jack stopped, looked around at everyone and took a breath. "I will repeat to you what he said in his statement. Obviously, the police will not take this part seriously, but I suspect you all will know more what to make of it than they." He swallowed a little nervously, looked around and continued.

"Siouxzy told Chuck that she magically changed herself into a cat, jumped into Shelly's car through the open window and hid until Tati discovered her a few blocks away. She, in her cat form fought off Tati and attacked Shelly's face and hands while she was driving, causing her to drive off the road."

Jen and Lorraine looked at one another and nodded. After Jen had told her mom about her vision after the excitement at Diane's place gone down, and Lorraine had confirmed that Officer Yardley noted scratches they found on Shelly's face when they recovered her body from Dead Man's Run. That wouldn't be proof enough for the police to definitively say that Siouxzy had caused Shelly's death, but it was enough for the Coven, and plans had been laid accordingly.

Everyone knew the spells keeping Siouxzy in place

wouldn't last. As soon as she was able, she would try to escape, and when that happened, the Coven was ready.

"Siouxzy told him that Shelly hit her head on the windshield and was unconscious when the car went into the creek. She and the dog escaped the vehicle, but Shelly did not," Jack said solemnly.

"Chuck said Siouxzy laid low for a bit and then stole a car – the VW Beetle recovered at Diane's farm, which was involved in a hit and run near Wesleyan campus on Friday morning, a half hour after it was reported stolen nearby." Jack said. "He stressed that she was a terrible driver.

The hit and run driver I'd witnessed that morning was Siouxzy. I didn't know if she knew I'd given her plates to the police, but I know it was only hours later that I saw her on the fence and she followed me and Bast home. I shuddered.

"She came by his place briefly for supplies and then disappeared. He said he didn't see her again until she showed up with Arthur on Saturday night and said she knew where the artifact was, but she needed backup. That's when they went to Diane's farm."

"We will, of course, continue the investigation as long as you direct us to. The firm has, as Miss Lisa can assure you, tenacious and well-connected investigators. They will find Siouxzy, if she can be found."

We already knew that the coroner had declared Shelly's cause of death as drowning, of course what the attorneys would have to prove would be that someone caused the accident. Pinning it to a cat would have been impossible, but they believed they could potentially put Siouxzy away for Viktor's murder at least, as well as her other criminal activity.

Just as soon as they could find her, that was.

Siouxzy had stayed in custody long enough to allow

her wounds heal up a little before she got ahold of someone who would smuggle in the ingredients she needed to refresh her transformation spell, and then, as far as the police could tell, she simply disappeared.

"And the stolen items?" Lorraine asked.

"With Charlotte's help, we've been able to create a list of the items Siouxzy took from Shelly's mother, with the exception of the item missing from the carved wooden box. Of course, if we could get a description of the item, it would make it more within the realm of possibility that we might be able to recover it," Jack said, a touch of frustration tinging his tone.

Someone coughed loudly from the back of the garage.

"Or maybe," I whispered to Jen, "Maybe there's someone here who can help with that."

Becky stood up and walked determinedly over to Dottie and Lorraine. She leaned down and whispered something in the air between them and Lorraine stood. She gave Becky a fierce hug and said to Lisa, "I believe the Coven has some private business to discuss, unless Jack has anything more that he wanted to share with us?"

"Just to say that while Chuck will be spending some quality time behind bars, Arthur has some extremely interesting attorneys who will keep him out and walking around while they play games with the court." Jack slipped his notes back into his briefcase and stood. "I don't know as much about Arthur, as he hasn't been a direct target of this investigation. But I know of these attorneys, and I'd like to stress to you all, their firm regularly represents some very dangerous people. Whatever you do with this item, should you happen to find it, be careful."

With that he took his leave of Lisa and closed the door behind him.

"Okay, Becky. Spill." Lorraine said gently.

Becky looked around at us short of sheepishly. "The reason the artifact wasn't in the wooden box when Diane dug it up is because I'd already stolen it. On Tuesday night, I was downtown at that dive bar on 9th Street and I heard Siouxzy. I couldn't see who she was talking to, but it must have been Viktor. She was on his ass about being a coward and owing her a favor and all this. Then I heard her say Shelly's name.

"I didn't know then that she was the one who'd gotten busted for stealing Shelly's mom's stuff, but when she said *Shelly*, I just got suspicious. I followed them out later, and then I got my car and drove by Shelly's place. Everything was totally fine. The next morning, Wednesday, I decided to swing by again, just to see, and that's when I saw her getting in her car with that plant. She seemed off, like she was looking over her shoulder and fumbling with her keys. So, I followed her.

"I figured out she was going to Diane's pretty quickly, and I doubled back around on that county road on the far side of Diane's fence, and I parked and got as close as I could to see what I could see."

I had this vision of Becky, wearing black ripped jeans, Vans and one of her Dead Kennedy's t-shirts, safety pins everywhere, long black hair in a dangerous ponytail, picking her way across the Nebraska prairie on an early morning in June.

"I saw her talking to Diane, and I saw her signal to Tati. Tati took off for the gate, Diane's dogs followed, I'm pretty sure Shelly undid the gate with a spell. At least she looked like she was casting from where I was at. Then she quick buried the box and planted the orchid right next to it. She was all done by the time Diane got back.

"I wasn't sure what was going on, but I knew if

Siouxzy was involved, there was the potential for extreme stupidity, and neither Shelly nor Diane needed that. So, I snuck in and took it and left the box."

"You opened it outside? On Tuesday, dear goddess, two days before the full moon." murmured Dottie.

"It was only exposed for a split second," Becky assured her, "and it was daylight. It's been completely under wraps since then, I haven't even looked at it. I figured I'd just keep it out of sight until everything cooled down and I could ask you guys what to do with it. But then after Siouxzy *escaped*, Arthur was released, so I thought maybe it should stay hidden."

"What the heck is this thing, anyway?" Rome demanded.

Dottie looked to me and held out a hand. "May I have a pen and paper, Angie? I know you're rarely without."

I scurried over and proffered the requested items. She took them and began to draw on a clean page. I watched, absorbed.

She drew a simple figure, a flat disc then three arcing arms. "It's an amulet, plain, even ugly in appearance. A flat metal piece with three arms that holds this," she drew in a center stone that was angular, like a few Legos stuck randomly together. She shaded it darkly. "It's a piece of a meteor that fell to the earth fairly recently, about 17 years ago, I believe," she said, eyeing me oddly. "It's dark in color, and metallic."

"Is it something like what Maka used on Jeanne?" I asked, thinking about the spell we'd helped Maka cast to transport Jeanne off planet before she could call the Pilgrims down on us.

"Not like that, but it does have some special aspects to it. We'll have to verify it, of course, but Maka thinks this meteor was in the sky from the Winter Solstice of 1969 until Autumnal equinox of 1970."

"Jen was born on the Winter Solstice of '69," I said frowning, "and I was born on the Autumnal equinox of 1970." I looked at Dottie. "David was born on the Spring equinox between us in May of '70." We knew this had something to do with our connection and our ability to focus the, what Maka called *the power of the triad.* Of course, whenever David said it, it sounded like something off a Saturday morning cartoon. It was what Lorraine and Lisa had been working on for months. I looked up and saw the two of them craning to have a look at the notebook page.

"Do you think this has something to do with *us?*" I asked Lorraine.

"Yes," she said simply.

"But what?" Jen asked.

"Ladies, sit down. I'm about to tell you a story," said Lisa. And she smiled.

THE END

Post Epilogue note:

For those of you, like my husband, who don't give a hoot about anybody in the story except for the dogs, it will please you to note that Miss Charlotte and David agreed to share custody of Tati. She spent weekdays with Charlotte and weekends with David through our senior year. Eventually, when he moved into a place of his own, Tati moved in with him full time. Charlotte insisted, saying Smokey liked being the only child anyway. Tati loved them both, but she agreed with Smokey and they all lived happily ever after.

The Zodiac Cusp Kids

♍︎♎︎ Angie Parsons 9/22/70 - Cusp of Beauty (Virgo/Libra) Musician, scholar. Necklace - blue. Dating Jon.

♉︎♊︎ David Owens 5/20/70 - Cusp of Energy (Taurus/Gemini) Athlete - football, then cross country after losing an eye in battle with Mitch. Necklace - green.

♐︎♑︎ Jen Howe 12/21/69 - Cusp of Prophecy (Sagittarius/-Capricorn) Twin sister to Jon. Actor in school theater productions. Has prophetic visions.

The Family

♐︎♑︎ Jon Howe 12/21/1969 - Cusp of Prophecy (Sagittarius/-Capricorn) Developing psychic 'sight' while losing his everyday sight. Twin brother to Jen. Dating Angie.

♊︎♋︎ Lorraine Howe Cusp of Magic (Gemini/Cancer) Jen and Jon's mom. Coven leader.

♒︎♓︎ Professor Alden Parsons Cusp of Sensitivity (Aquarius/Pisces) - Angie's dad. The Guardian.

♌︎♍︎ Elizabeth Parsons Cusp of Exposure (Leo/Virgo) - Angie's mom.

♎︎ Mallory Parsons Angie's older sister.

♋︎ Donna Owens David's mom. In car accident with Mitch (Something Wicked) and suffered traumatic brain injury. Never recovered completely & lived in nursing home. Was possessed by Jeanne's magic (Something Twisted) which ultimately led to her passing.

Fellow Adventurers

♈♉ **Mr. Rakow** — Vietnam veteran. Neighbor to David's mom, Donna. Friend to Lorraine and the Parsons.

♑♒ **Maka (The Grandmother)** — Advisor to Lorrain, Rakow and the Parsons. Powerful magic user.

♏♐ **Malinowski** — Orphaned in an attack on his moon. Rescued by and is companion/journeyman to Maka (Something Found.) In a relationship with Barb.

♓♈ **Barb** — Troubled kid, living in group home at Whitehall. Got involved with the Zodiac Cusp Kids when her friend's sister was kidnapped. Taken on as apprentice to Maka after the events of Something Lost. In a relationship with Malinowski.

The Coven

♊ **Shelly** — Grew up in Lincoln. Returned after college to care for aging mother. Ex-bf is Viktor. Best friends with Miss Charlotte. Dog: Tati. Magic color: Deep rose.

♉ **Lisa** — Local to Nebraska. Family owns much land and invested well. Teaches ad hoc classes at the University. Apprenticed to Maka. Knits constantly. Adept with abundance spells. Expert at amplifying spell intensity. Girlfriend: Nicole. Magic Color: Wheat gold.

♏ **Nicole** — Originally from Salem, Mass. Recently changed jobs from the University Library to the Public Library - filled the opening left by Jeanne's exit in Something Twisted. Current Girlfriend: Lisa. Ex-girlfriend: Pat. Working with Elizabeth on managing familiars. Expert at Rune magic. Magic color: ocean blue.

♈ Rome   Originally from Kansas. Assistant Manager at local retro diner. Fabric designer and seamstress. Expert at designing spells, works with Deanne and Lisa to craft new spells for the Coven. Magic color: Fuchsia

♓ Deanne   Local to Nebraska. Works as archivist at the local newspaper. Emotional caretaker of the coven. Rescues troubled cats. Expert at grasping the potential complexities of new spell creation. Has some empathic abilities, enhanced by magic. Magic color: sky blue

♒ Becky   Recently graduated high school. Plays drums in the punk band, Skurge Puppies. Was observed by Dottie shoplifting using magic. Was given help and training from the Coven on controlling her use of magic. Expert at sensory magic, including invisibility spells. Magic color: deep blue

♏ Elizabeth   Junior at UNL studying anthropology and political science. Aspiring novelist. Expert at working with complex, many-stage spells. Adept at working with familiars, particularly cats. Magic color: deep purple

♊ Diane   Master Gardiner, has an acreage outside of town where she's curated a large fenced prairie garden. Also has a farm near Lawrence, KS. Expert at working with botanical magics. Three dogs: Bailey, Jim and Huck. Magic color: forest green

♐ Ginny   Young mom of three. Lives with her mother who taught her magic. Adept at working with creative energies. Animal lover - de facto home to all neighborhood strays. Expert at multiplying power across members of the spellcasting group. Boyfriend: Chuck. Magic color: new leaf green

♊	Jules	PhD student, frequent traveler, part time scientist. Adept at micro magic - spells that exerted tiny changes at critical levels in a system. Expert at identifying and working with stones to assist in working the Coven's magic. Boyfriend: Aurthur. Magic color: sun-blasted sand
♑	Dottie	Oldest coven member. Retired Art--History professor. Friends with Angie's dad and Shelly's mom. Adept at group magic. Expert at detecting tiny flaws capable of derailing destructive magic spells. Magic color: pure silver
♌	Pat	Nicole's ex. PhD student in Genetics. Bartender at a seedy downtown dive. Adept at detecting concealment spells. Expert at digging up long lost spells and lore. Magic color: grey/black

The Pack

Shadow	German Shepherd. He/him. Human: Mr. Rakow
Bast	Siamese. HRH. Human: Answers to no one. Sometimes chooses to loo
Tati	Yellow English Lab. She/her. Human: Shelly
Alesta	German Shepherd. She/her. Human: Barb
Bailey, Jim and Huck	English Shepherds. Bailey: she/her, Jim & Huck: he/him Human: Diane
Smokey	Cat. Gray/brown tabby. He/him. Human: Charlotte

The Neighborhood

| Officer Yardley | Neighborhood Lincoln Police Department officer. Can also see some of the things Mr. Rakow and the Zodiac Cusp Kids see. Assists in most cases where anything hinky might be going on. Slayed Great Dane-sized spiders at the mall with Mr. Rakow in Something Twisted |

Miss Jeanne	Former Wesleyan student of Professor Parsons. Former librarian at the neighborhood branch. Disappears after the events of *Something Twisted*.
Miss Charlotte	Downtown Librarian. Has worked with Angie often on research projects. Best friends with Shelly. Cat: Smokey
Clint	Jen's 1971 Brown Chevy Impala. Seatbelts for six. Theoretical space for nine.

Trouble

Viktor	Shelly's ex-boyfriend. History of stalking.
Arthur	Jules's boyfriend. Drives a Trans-Am.
Chuck	Ginny's boyfriend. Breeds dogs. Drives a truck. Regular at Rome's diner
Siouxzy	Former in-home health aide to Shelly's mom.

Something Wicked
the First Tale of the Zodiac Cusp Kids

It's 1983. Angie, Jenny, and David are watching MTV, riding bikes, and looking forward to summer vacation before they start junior high school. Lincoln, Nebraska is a pretty quiet place to grow up, and when the kids take off at 5:00 am to deliver newspapers on Jenny's route, they aren't expecting trouble. So, when a creature straight out of a horror movie appears, the kids are forced to draw on their wits, their strengths, and most of all their friendship to survive.

Something Haunted
the Second Tale of the Zodiac Cusp Kids

The summer of 1983 is over. After weeks of healing from their first adventure and some specialized basic training with Mr. Rakow, Angie, Jenny and David are feeling prepared for the horrors junior high will surely bring. The final weekend of vacation, a bizarre tornado tears through Lincoln, upending gravestones and depositing supernatural debris on the school grounds. The gang has their hands full with the demands of starting junior high on top of trying to figure out an otherworldly mystery, and their friendship begins to feel the strain. But the malevolent ghost haunting the school is ramping up its attacks on students, and the kids are going to have to get it together in time to save the school.

Something Lost
the Third Tale of the Zodiac Cusp Kids

It's a Friday afternoon in the spring of 1985, when Crystal and Barb, two girls from Whitehall, the neighborhood group home for troubled kids, approach Angie at school. Crystal's little sister has disappeared, and her foster parents and the police think she's just another runaway. Crystal doesn't believe it, and when she and Barb learn there's a ghost involved, they know they're going to need the kind of help Angie, David and Jenny have developed a reputation for.

The Zodiac Cusp Kids enlist some extra help from Jen's twin Jon and a couple of very special German Shepherd pups to uncover what has really happened to Crystal's sister, and what they find is darker and more complex than anyone imagined.

Something Found
the Fourth Tale of the Zodiac Cusp Kids

Just over a week has passed since Angie, David and Jenny said goodbye to Barb and Alesta, the German Shepherd pup when David and Jenny convince Jon and Angie to come to a dance at the neighborhood Rec

Center. Mysterious things begin to appear as soon as the girls start getting ready for the dance. Jenny's prophecies guide them to a magical artifact that transports the Zodiac Cusp Kids away from the dance on a world-hopping rescue that opens their eyes to a terrifying new enemy, and to some powerful magical allies closer to home than they'd dreamed.

Something Found is the fourth of seven stories drawn from Angie's diaries. Kept safely hidden for decades, they tell how the kids spent their teenage years — working with their mentor, Mr. Rakow, and Jenny's mom, Lorraine, who dabbles in witchcraft, to realize their power and battle the forces of darkness that menace their hometown.

Something Twisted
the Fifth Tale of the Zodiac Cusp Kids

Two years have passed since Angie, David, and Jenny returned from their star-hopping adventure and learned the identity of the Guardian. Now sophomores in high school, the kids are trying to juggle saving their hometown while also having social lives, playing on sports teams, acting in plays, and studying healing magic outside of class. When those worlds begin to collide with dangerous magic, the kids have their hands full figuring out who to trust. Then, David's mom gets dragged into the mess and the Guardian puts his relationship with the whole team on the line to discover the identity of the culprit. Plus, Great Dane-sized-spiders. Hold onto your hats, Something Twisted is going on!

Something Fatal
the Sixth Tale of the Zodiac Cusp Kids

1987 is a rough year for Angie, David and Jen. Just weeks after the tragic passing of David's mom, one of the members of Lorraine's coven goes missing. Untangling the web of lies, thievery and intrigue surrounding her misadventure is a challenge fit for Agatha Christie. Unless Angie and the others can figure out who is responsible for Shelly's death, the emotional and magical well-being of the entire Coven is at risk, and that bodes ill for everyone in the state of Nebraska and beyond.

Something Final
the Last Tale of the Zodiac Cusp Kids

Coming September 7, 2021

About the Author

Sarah Dale is an author, mom, partner, daughter, step-mom, friend, dog-walker, cat-appreciator, library book-balancer, word lover, think-thinker and picture-taker living in Lincoln, Nebraska, and just generally trying to get things done.

www.sarahdaleauthor.com

Facebook: facebook.com/wecouldbeheroesnovel/

Twitter: @sarahdaleauthor

Instagram: instagram.com/wecouldbeheroesnovel/

Goodreads: goodreads.com/stillphoenix

Amazon: amazon.com/author/stillphoenix

Other titles you might enjoy from Snowy Wings Publishing

Sing, Goddess!
-Jane Watson, ed.
https://www.snowywingspublishing.com/book/sing-goddess/

A Spark in Space
-Janina Franck
https://www.snowywingspublishing.com/book/a-spark-in-space/

Detours
-Amy Bearce
https://www.snowywingspublishing.com/book/detours/